MIKHAIL BARYSHNIKOV'S

STORIES
From My
CHILDHOOD

BELOVED FAIRY TALES FROM
"THE SNOW QUEEN" TO
"IVAN AND HIS MAGIC PONY"
TO "CINDERELLA"

For those who raised us and gave us the ability to see the world
as good and wise and gentle

Varvara Ivanovna and Boris Nikolievich
Orin and Laura
Aunt Nuta
Irina Alexandrovna

For our son
Sergei

And to all of the talented directors, artists, writers, and workers
of Soyuzmultfilm Studio, Moscow

—J.B. and O.V.

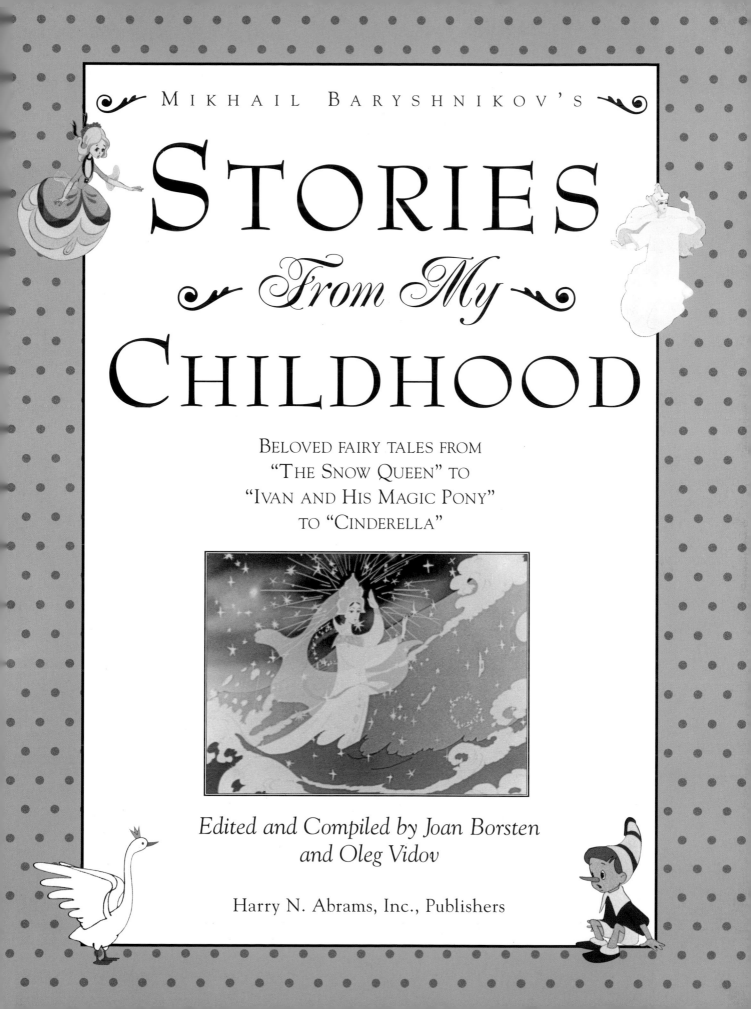

MIKHAIL BARYSHNIKOV'S

STORIES *From My* CHILDHOOD

BELOVED FAIRY TALES FROM
"THE SNOW QUEEN" TO
"IVAN AND HIS MAGIC PONY"
TO "CINDERELLA"

*Edited and Compiled by Joan Borsten
and Oleg Vidov*

Harry N. Abrams, Inc., Publishers

ACKNOWLEDGMENTS

We wish to thank some of the people who have made possible the animated series "Mikhail Baryshnikov's Stories From My Childhood," including The Audrey Hepburn Children's Fund, Sean Ferrer, Arnie Messer, Lisa Rinehart, Leeza Vinnichenko, Nikolai Tarasov, Michael J. Solomon, Rick Mischel, Roman Konbrandt, Stanislav Roshkov, Rimma Erohkina, Mila Straupe, Sonia Konbrandt, Regina Billings, Melissa Wohl, Valerie Allen, Richard and Francesca Harrison, and the Marian Sriencz family.

A very special thanks to Mikhail Baryshnikov and Mike Medavoy.

And those who have made possible this book, including our agent, Deborah Grosvenor, and Howard Reeves and Emily Farbman of Harry N. Abrams, Inc., Publishers.

As well as those who over the years have helped us piece together the history of Soyuzmultfilm, including Fyodor Khitruk, Yuri Norstein, Irina Margolina, Eduard Nazarov, Anatoly Volkov, and Georgi Borodin.

Designer: Sonia Chaghatzbanian
Production Director: Hope Koturo

Library of Congress Cataloging-in-Publication Data

Vidov, Oleg
Mikhail Baryshnikov's stories from my childhood: beloved fairy tales from The snow queen to Ivan and his magic pony to Cinderella / by Oleg Vidov and Joan Borsten Vidov.
p. cm.
Based on the animated series, "Mikhail Baryshnikov's stories from my childhood."
Summary: A collection of eleven fairy tales by a variety of authors including "The Golden Rooster" by Alexander Pushkin and "The Wild Swans" by Hans Christian Andersen, as well as traditional tales such as "Cinderella" and "Twelve Months."
ISBN 0-8109-1017-9
1. Fairy tales. [1. Fairy tales.] I. Borsten Vidov, Joan. II. Title.

PZ8.V58 Mi 2002
[Fic]—dc21
2002018308

Printed and bound in Singapore

10 9 8 7 6 5 4 3 2 1

Harry N. Abrams, Inc.
100 Fifth Avenue
New York, N.Y. 10011
www.abramsbooks.com

Abrams is a subsidiary of

LA MARTINIÈRE
GROUPE

Table of Contents

Foreword

Growing up in the Soviet republic of Latvia in the early 1950s, Saturdays and Sundays were children's days at the local movie houses. Full-length features, shorts, and cartoons played all afternoon, and whole families came ready to shake off the grimness of the work week. In the better theaters, the lobby was arranged with comfortable chairs and a small orchestra played classical music and popular tunes. Better yet, concession stands were stocked with stacks of sandwiches, ice-cream bars, and barley-sugar pops molded into animal shapes. After checking our coats at the door—the event was special enough to dress up for—I'd tug my mother's hand and head straight for the shiny glass cases to choose a treat. My favorite, a sweet, fizzy concoction of ice, seltzer, and syrup, could be nursed to last the full fifteen or twenty minutes it took for the orchestra to work through its repertoire. And this was before we even entered the theater! Needless to say, if I could convince my parents to get me there, my day was made.

After the music, we'd go into the actual movie house and wait for the lights to dim. Even then, the hushed anticipation of darkened space meant magic. And what magic! The stories I'd absorbed from toddlerhood in my mother's voice, and later from well-thumbed, beautifully illustrated volumes, burst onto the screen like giant flip books alive with sound and movement.

Suddenly, the handsome prince had a voice, the maiden a bashful glance, and the nasty queen an imperious sweep of cloak. The familiar two-dimensional characters of my earliest memories became instantly larger, brighter, and more powerful. Caught up in the drama, I'd yell with the rest of the children as we called out support for the virtuous characters and castigation for their enemies.

My mother preferred the theater and ballet, but she never minded these trips to the movies, no matter how messy or noisy they got. She'd grown up with the same stories and trusted the lessons embedded in them. To her, the films were simply another opening to a world where good conquers evil, where humility and patience are beyond price, and where the wise and brave always win.

As a parent, I now understand her indulgence. These folktales, on the screen or on the page, are as potent today as ever. With their strong moral structure and exotic mystery, they are edifying *and* enticing—no easy task in storytelling. What's more, just as the stories came alive for me on the screen in Riga, the capital of Latvia, they are illuminated and enriched in this book by glorious artwork taken from the animated films. Clearly, the virtuosity of the Soyuzmultfilm artists has stood the test of time. I am happy and proud to pass on these tales to my children, knowing, although their world is very different from what I knew as a child, they, too, can wander in magical realms, where the finest human attributes are the most rewarded. ✳

—*Mikhail Baryshnikov*

Beauty and the Beast

A Tale of the Crimson Flower

Once upon a time there lived a merchant. He sought after riches that were the finest in the world, treasures from over the seas. He lived with his three daughters, all fair and loving toward their father. They were more beloved to him than all his wealth, but he loved his youngest daughter best, for her generosity and love for him were the most pure.

One day as the merchant was preparing to travel to faraway lands, he called his daughters to him and said, "While I am away, I want only one thing from my daughters. Listen to me, girls. You must find a way to live together in peace and harmony, with no bickering and no fighting—only love. If you will do this for me, I will bring you back anything you wish." He turned to his eldest daughter and said, "What will you have me bring you, Natalia?"

"Oh, let me think!" Natalia replied. "I want a crown like no one else has ever had, covered in jewels—rubies and diamonds—and of solid gold, so people will say of me, 'Is she not beautiful?'"

The merchant chuckled and said, "You shall have your beautiful crown, Natalia. And what shall I bring back for you, my pretty Parasha?"

"I don't know, not much," the merchant's middle daughter answered coyly. "Only a trifle I've heard about. It's a magic mirror that when you look into it, there you are forever young. In it, I will never look old but always young and pretty."

The merchant spoke to Parasha. "You will always be pretty to me, mirror or not." Then, turning to his youngest daughter, he asked, "And what of you, Anastasia?"

Anastasia told her father, "All I need is your safe return."

"But I want to bring a gift to you," the merchant insisted.

And so the youngest daughter began to describe her desired gift. "Once in a dream I saw a flower, crimson red and unusual, with a sadness about it. If you find such a flower, that may be my gift." Anastasia's sisters mocked her foolishness.

"A sad flower?" laughed Parasha.

"That's ridiculous," agreed Natalia.

As his ship set sail, the merchant called good-bye to his daughters

and promised he would return with their wishes. The merchant
sailed to strange countries, across seas he had never traveled. He
traded his goods and collected many riches in return. He found the
gifts for his middle and oldest daughters, but could not find the
crimson flower of which Anastasia spoke. On a stormy night, still
riding the glowing sea, the merchant's crew urged him to turn for
home, predicting the coming winds.

"I cannot return," the merchant cried. "I have no gift for lovely
Anastasia. I have promised her the crimson flower." As the skies grew
darker and the sea became rougher and rougher, the crew worked
hard to keep the ship steady. Suddenly a huge, strong wave crashed
into the ship. The merchant lost his balance and was washed into the
sea. When he awoke, the merchant found he was lying on the beach
of a shimmering island unlike any land he had ever seen.

"Remarkable!" he said to himself as he entered a lush forest.
"Perhaps I have reached the end of the world. If the crimson flower
does exist, this is surely the place I'll find it." As he walked through

the strange and beautiful woodland, he came to a clear pool of water, beyond which was a magnificent palace. "So I am not alone on this island," he thought. "The master of this house must be very rich and powerful." As the merchant stood, wondering how to cross the water, a boat appeared, as if it knew his thoughts. He took the boat across to the palace and walked up its grand steps.

"Hello," he called as he reached a great set of doors. Again, as if in response, they opened. The inside of the palace was even more marvelous than the outside. The merchant's voice echoed as he called out to whoever might live there. He sat to rest and thought about how long it had been since he last had a hearty meal. Suddenly, a table appeared, covered with gold and silver dishes filled with steaming foods and cool drinks. The contented merchant enjoyed the unusual food and drink. He toasted the kind and invisible host to show his thanks for providing such

a delicious meal. He rose from the table, and no sooner had he risen than the table disappeared.

The merchant was enchanted and continued to wander through the sumptuous palace. Shortly he came across a blooming flower surrounded by a radiant aura of light. It was a crimson flower of unbelievable beauty, so astonishing that the merchant's heart skipped a beat. He exclaimed in joy, "At last I have found the crimson flower for my precious Anastasia!"

With these words, he plucked the flower. At that moment, lightning flashed and thunder crashed and the trees were tossed by a strong wind. Through the bending trees, the merchant saw the strange figure of a huge and terrible monster. He heard the beast roar in a frightening voice, "What have you done? How dare you take my flower? I welcomed you and gave you every comfort in my humble home. Yet you repay me by taking my greatest joy. For this, you must die!"

The merchant trembled and whispered, "I am not afraid to die. I took the flower because I promised it to my youngest daughter, Anastasia."

"Your youngest daughter, Anastasia," the Beast repeated. "What a kind and loving daughter she must be to have earned such fierce devotion. For her, I will let you live. You may leave my island and take the crimson flower. But you must give your solemn promise that one of your daughters will return in your place. I will not harm her. She will be well cared for."

"Never!" the merchant cried, and wept bitter tears. "You do not know a father's heart!"

The Beast replied, "Someone must pay for your transgression. Someone must return here to be my companion, or you must die. I will give you a ring. Whoever places it on her finger will return instantly to me. If it is not one of your daughters, then it must be you. I can live in loneliness no longer."

The merchant accepted the ring with a heavy heart. Just then the merchant's crew found their way to the Beast's island, collected their captain, and began the journey home.

The merchant returned to his home to find his daughters thrilled to see their father. Natalia and Parasha admired their wonderful gifts, but Anastasia was the most touched to have been given the flower of her dreams. Evening came and she sat with her knitting beside the shimmering flower. From the next room, she overheard her father quietly speaking with his first mate about his promise to return to the beast. "I gave my word, my promise," he explained. "The ship is yours, and I entrust to you the care of my beloved daughters. I took the Beast's flower, and I must pay the price. At sunrise, I must put on the ring and return to the island."

"Oh, Father," Anastasia said to herself. "What have I done to you? My foolish request made you take the crimson flower. My silly desire caused you to stir the wrath of the vengeful Beast. So I must be the one to pay." Anastasia rose from her work and went in search of the ring

in her father's room. The moment Anastasia put the ring on her finger, her father awoke from his sleep to see his beloved daughter disappear before his eyes. "Father," she called to him, "forgive your foolish daughter."

"Anastasia!" he called after her, but she was already transported to the Beast's island.

"It's so beautiful," Anastasia said, marveling as she looked around. "Surely no beast could live here." She was surrounded by brilliant cascading waterfalls and a rainbow of colorful flowers. Playful animals scampered around her feet. "The animals do not seem to be afraid of anything," thought Anastasia. "Why should I be?"

She still held the crimson flower in her hand, but it suddenly rose from her grasp and returned to its original flower bed. As it settled back in, Anastasia heard the voice of the beast.

"Thank you, Anastasia. My greatest joy has come to me at last."

"I am sorry," Anastasia said. "My father took it because of me."

"I know why your father took it," the Beast replied with understanding. "And in return I wish only for you to stay here with me. I will give you whatever you need. You shall have the finest gowns and robes in all the world." With that, Anastasia found herself clothed in a magnificent dress.

"Go look in the mirror," the Beast urged her. A tall mirror appeared within the waterfall, and Anastasia gazed at her reflection as her clothes changed before her eyes, each gown more and more beautiful than the one before.

"Thank you for your kindness," Anastasia said, laughing, "but I prefer my own clothes. They are simple, as I am."

"As you wish, Anastasia," the Beast said. "I have no desire to

punish you. I wish only for your happiness. This island, all that is here, is yours to share. All I ask in return is that you treat me with the same compassion you give to all living things. I welcome you here not as a guest, but as an equal. You are now the mistress of this house."

Time passed, and Anastasia enjoyed all the beautiful things that the island and her host offered her. But sometimes she missed her home so strongly and grew lonely for her father and sisters. One day, knowing that he could hear her, Anastasia spoke to the Beast.

"It seems that you're not the beast my father spoke of after all. Why do you not show yourself?" she asked.

"I must always remain invisible," he replied. "But it is my dearest hope that you will bring laughter and song back into my house. Your kind heart and beauty already put to shame the riches of my palace."

"Thank you for everything, dear friend," Anastasia said as she looked at the wonders that surrounded her. "It is all wonderful. But I long to return to my loving father and sisters. I miss them so much. Please accept your ring." Sadly, Anastasia held out the ring, hoping the Beast would take it.

"Keep it," the Beast answered. "Its magic is very powerful, and yours to control. With it, you may return home whenever you wish. I cannot hold you here when your desire to visit your family is so strong. But remember, your father promised I would not be alone. If you go, I do not know what I will do without you."

Anastasia thought about what the Beast had said as she wandered through her new home. While she sat by the waterfall and thought, the Beast longed to make her happy. Bravely, he crept nearer to her than he had ever come before. He wished he could comfort her, but he worried that his frightening appearance would terrify her.

He crept too close. Anastasia looked up from her thoughts to find the Beast peering out at her from behind the trees. Seeing him, she

gasped in horror and hid her face. The Beast hung his head in shame. "I have frightened you, Anastasia. Now you will leave me forever!"

Anastasia realized that though the Beast was frightening to see, she had grown fond of him. She had never met such a generous being. "Forgive me," she said to him as she searched in the shadows for his figure. "I am a fool and I did not mean to hurt you. You are my dearest friend. Please, appear to me again and I swear by my heart I will not be frightened."

"No, Anastasia," the Beast spoke. "You are repulsed by the sight of me. I cannot blame you. I am no more than a lonely wretched beast. You could never accept an ugly creature like me into your heart. You have the power of the ring. Use it to fly away from me, and alone I will die of grief."

"I promise I will not leave you," Anastasia said. "Not if it will hurt you. I am content here, and I do care for you."

"If only I could believe," she heard the Beast say.

Time passed, and after a time, Anastasia again shared with the Beast her desire to return home to see her family.

"I wish only for your happiness, Anastasia," the Beast told her. "Use the ring to go home to visit your family. I beg you only return to me by sunset, or I will waste away without you."

Anastasia quickly returned to her father and sisters, who were overjoyed to see her. Natalia and Parasha were amazed at her beautiful dress and how happy and healthy she looked.

"What did you bring for us?" Natalia asked.

"Yes, where are the gifts?" echoed Parasha.

As they said this, beside each of them appeared a chest full of beautiful dresses and fine jewels. Delighted, Anastasia's sisters looked at every beautiful item while Anastasia spoke with her father.

"I've missed you all so much," said Anastasia. "But the Beast is very kind and generous. In his kindness, he willingly sent me back. He has such a good heart, but it is heavy with loneliness—I don't know why. I promised I would return by sunset."

"How clever you are, sister," said Natalia, who had overheard her sister's words. "To trick the stupid Beast into letting you go!"

"And taking all these treasures with you!" said Parasha.

"But I never thought to deceive him," said Anastasia. "If I am not back by sunset, I am sure he will die of grief. I must return to him."

Seeing all the beautiful things that Anastasia was given by the Beast, her sisters

were jealous. Their envy of their sister was so strong that they could not even stand the thought of Anastasia returning to the wonderful palace and the Beast's generosity. They secretly turned back all of the clocks and shuttered the windows.

As the family sat around the dinner table, Anastasia began to feel strange and worried. "My heart is pounding," she said. "Something is not right. I feel I should return to the island."

"Why do you worry so?" asked Parasha. "It's not even seven yet."

"That's strange," said their father. "It seems late. It's quite dark in here. Why are the windows shuttered? Who did this?"

"Oh, it was so cold," the sisters replied, laughing.

Anastasia opened the window and gasped in fear, seeing that the sun had left the sky. "It's already dark! He will think I've betrayed him! Sisters, why have you done this?" Quickly, she slipped on the ring. When she returned to the island, the sky was dark and stormy. The trees were being tossed by powerful winds.

"Beast, Beast! Where are you?" Anastasia called. "Why are you not answering me? I have returned, my gentle friend. Please forgive me!" She struggled through the stormy forest and came across the Beast, lying helpless on the ground. "Oh, my dearest friend," she said, weeping, "what have I done? You must not die, I beg you. I love you, my lonely Beast."

As she knelt beside the Beast, Anastasia's tears fell on the wilted crimson flower that the Beast clutched in his hand. As the drops struck, the flower began to bloom again. Before her eyes, the Beast awoke and began to transform into a handsome young prince. Confused, Anastasia stepped back from the figure.

"Anastasia!" the handsome man called. "Do not run from me. You looked into my heart and loved me when I appeared to be a beast. I need you to love me still, as the man I really am." He stood before her, still holding the crimson flower.

"I do love you," said Anastasia, "for who you are inside."

"For years I've lived alone and ugly on this island," the prince explained, "because a witch who hated my good fortune put a spell on me. As a beast, I was forced by this terrible sorceress to live until a gentle beauty could look beyond my ugly face and see into my heart. You are that beauty, Anastasia." The prince gave her the blooming flower. "And the evil spell is broken forever. We will be together now, for truly the beauty of your heart has transformed this humble Beast." And Anastasia and her loving prince lived happily ever after. ❧

The Golden Rooster

In a realm long ago, in a faraway kingdom, ruled the illustrious Czar Dadon. He had spent his younger days as a strong leader, invading the lands of his enemies. But he had grown old and weary of fighting and wanted to live in peace. Those the czar had once attacked saw an opportunity to take their revenge. They attacked again and again, keeping the frontiers of the empire under constant threat.

Dadon's generals were frequently caught off guard. For

instance, whenever they expected an attack to come from the south, the enemy invaded in the east. Exhausted with the battles, the czar gathered his sons and nobles to seek their advice. During their meeting, a mysterious magician arrived and sought the czar's attention. Out of his bag he pulled a golden rooster, which he gave to Dadon with some words of advice.

"Place this rooster on the weather vane atop your highest tower. He will be your faithful guardian, keeping watch over your land. If all is peaceful in your domain, he will not move. But at the slightest threat of war, the slightest menace of invasion, the rooster will raise his head, cry out in alarm, and turn to face the danger."

The czar thanked the magician and wished to reward him with gold, but the magician refused.

"Well, then, since you have rendered me such a service," said the czar, "I shall grant your dearest wish as though it were my own. You have my word."

The rooster, perched high atop a tower, waited for a threat to launch his cry. At the smallest sign of danger, this faithful bird awoke, fluttered his wings, turned toward the peril, and cried:

"Kiri-koo-koo! Long live the czar whose word is true!"

Word of the czar's well-guarded kingdom spread far and wide. The czar's warlike neighbors no longer dared attack the mighty leader. Time passed calmly, free of care. The rooster no longer stirred.

One day Dadon was wakened by a loud noise.

"Czar Dadon! Great czar, awaken!" one of his generals shouted. "There is danger!"

"What?" asked Dadon, yawning. "What is this awful commotion?"

The general answered, "Look, sire! The rooster has crowed and now turns to the east."

The Czar dashed to his window.

The rooster, fluttering in agitation, was pointing toward the east. "Kiri-koo-koo! Long live the czar whose word is true!"

"There is no time to lose," called Dadon to his soldiers. "To your horses!"

Dadon's army, led by his elder son, set out to battle the eastern enemy.

For eight days the bird made no sound, and the czar heard no news.

Finally, the rooster sang once more toward the east, and the czar raised another army. This time he decided to send his younger son on a rescue mission.

Another week passed without news of the second army! When the rooster crowed a third time, the czar raised a third army, over which he personally took command.

The army rode day and night with no sign of battle. They found no camps or graves, nor friend or foe.

Then, on the eighth day, the army chose a dark path down a mountain. At the bottom of the narrow gorge the czar came upon the remains of his two armies and the slain bodies of his sons.

"Oh! What horror has happened here?" Dadon moaned.

"My only sons! My two brave falcons pierced and fallen from the sky. I shall die from grief!"

The czar's general and soldiers swore revenge on the enemy who had left no trace. Then, before their eyes, a tent appeared with twinkling stars shimmering at the top. A young woman, mysterious and beautiful, the princess of Shamakhan, appeared before the czar. He gazed at the radiant young maid and immediately forgot that his sons were dead. Bewitched by her charms, the czar entered her tent and remained with her for a week. Each day he grew more enchanted with her and finally begged her to be his wife, promising her all his riches.

At last the czar set out to return to his kingdom with the princess. When he arrived, Dadon was welcomed by loud

cheers. As he looked out over the crowd, he noticed the magician who had given him the golden rooster.

"Hello, my magical friend," Dadon said to him. "Is there some favor you wish to ask of me?"

"As I gave you the golden rooster, you gave to me your solemn word that you would fulfill one wish of mine as if it were your own," the magician said.

"That is so," agreed the czar, bowing.

The magician nodded. "In payment of your debt, then, I demand the princess of Shamakhan, your bride, for my own."

"How dare you demand such a thing of me, you greedy devil!" the czar cried in astonishment. "Just for that, you'll get nothing! Guards! Go and seize this evil wretch!"

"You have gone back on your word!" cried the angry magician.

Dadon spat in fury and shouted, "Still you argue? Truly, you are your own worst enemy!"

The czar brandished his cane and struck the magician on the forehead. As the man fell, the rooster rose from the weathervane and called out, "Kiri-koo-koo, shame to those whose word is not true." The rooster flew down with a flutter of wings. He landed on Dadon's head, which he split open with one huge peck. The princess of Shamakhan laughed wickedly and vanished as if she had never existed.

There is a lesson in this tale: Live wisely and kindly, and always keep your word.

The Snow Queen

In an old crowded town where beautiful gardens grew in little tiny spaces, there lived two children who had a rose garden somewhat larger than a flowerpot. They cared for each other as much as if they were brother and sister. His name was Kai, hers was Gerta, and they knew they would be friends forever, never apart. When the freezing cold air came down from the north and the autumn rain turned to snow, Kai would spend the long winter evenings in Gerta's house. Her grandmother would tell them all kinds of stories about the world.

"We are so lucky to have such a warm house on such a cold night," Gerta's grandmother began. "Ah, look. The first winter snow. And every snowflake looks like a white bee. Do you know where they come from?"

"Far to the north, past the cold seas and blinding fog," she continued, "into the frozen winds that lead to the land of bitter storms and deadly blizzards. That is the home of those snowflakes—all of them servants of the Snow Queen."

"The Snow Queen?" Gerta whispered.

"Yes," her grandmother told her. "In the far north, where the snow never melts, is a magnificent castle made of the coldest ice, sparkling in the northern lights. This is where the Snow Queen lives."

"Is she beautiful?" asked Kai.

"She is so beautiful, it makes you shiver," the grandmother answered. "She shines like the Polar Star, alone and elusive. Hurt by a burning love, she became as cold as the ice that always surrounds her, and now she walks the large halls of her wondrous palace alone. There are rooms filled with treasures, but none are as important to her as her magic mirror. Through this mirror she can see into her vast winter kingdom. You must know that in the spring, as the snow melts and the earth is bare, the Snow Queen becomes weak. So she must expand her kingdom as much as possible in the winter. She does this by watching, watching everyone who does not obey her demands. Her biggest threat of all are those who have warm hearts."

As she heard her grandmother say this, Gerta noticed the

face of the Snow Queen through the icy window-pane. "Look," she gasped, "she's watching us!"

"Gerta! She can't get in," Kai reassured his friend. "And if she did, I would put her on a hot stove and she'd melt!"

The Snow Queen overheard the boy say this and returned to her palace in anger. "Arrogant boy!" she exclaimed. "He is challenging me!" In her anger she struck her magic mirror, which broke into shards. "Fly, shards," she commanded, "as sharp as darts. Pierce the heart of the boy who dares to judge me. Pierce his eye so he sees no beauty. Pierce his heart so that it freezes and he feels no love. When this is done, he will not be Kai, he will be all mine!"

That night, Kai and Gerta watched the blustering storm from inside the warm house. As they looked toward the window, it suddenly burst open, letting the wind swirl in, carrying the sharp, icy shards sent by the Snow Queen.

"Oh! I feel a sharp pain in my heart," Kai cried. "And now something has got into my eye!"

Gerta rushed to his side to have a look. Kai pushed her aside and coldly said, "It's nothing. It fell out already." But the shards had not fallen out. They were pieces of cold crystal from the Snow Queen's magic mirror, and already they were turning Kai's heart into ice. He began to treat his dear friend Gerta with cruelty.

The next day, Kai did not invite Gerta to play with his sled. He finally let her join him, but set off on the sled at such a speed that Gerta could not stay on. "I knew you would fall off, crybaby," he teased her. He proudly walked off without her into the town square, where children would hitch their sleds to the fast carts. When he arrived, he saw the Snow Queen drive up in her icy sleigh led by silvery horses. The children scattered out of her way.

"Are you brave enough to attach to my sleigh, Kai?" she asked the boy. "You would go faster than all the boys. Come with me, Kai. I'll show you an enchanting palace no one has ever seen. Come!"

Gerta saw her friend attach his sled to the Snow Queen's sleigh, and she called, "Kai! It's the Snow Queen. It's a spell!" But Kai ignored her and was whisked away to the Snow Queen's icy kingdom.

After they had traveled quite a distance, the Snow Queen stopped and looked back at Kai. "Do you still think you can melt me on a hot stove, Kai?" she asked. She saw him shivering and said, "You are cold, little one. Come to me." She kissed the boy's forehead.

"Your kiss is cold, so cold it hurts," Kai said.

"I won't kiss you anymore," said the Snow Queen. "Soon you will not even feel the cold. You must trust me, brave Kai. My love is peaceful and safe. You will never be bothered by troubles. I am going to take you to a beautiful palace. You will be the prince in my kingdom and forget everything about this life. Feelings only destroy people. It is best to be above everything, as I am, my brave prince. Your heart will soon be as hard as diamonds. You will not know joy, but you will also not know

sadness. You will feel nothing. You will be like me, not happy or sad. You will not care about anything or anyone. In this you will find contentment."

Winter passed, seasons changed, and Kai never returned to the little town. Of course, everyone thought the worst. Everyone but Gerta, who, in spring, when the Snow Queen's power weakened, took her new shoes, kissed her grandmother good-bye, and went off in search of her dearest friend. She did not know where to go and decided to ask the river for help.

"River, river, please tell me, do you know where the Snow Queen lives? I would gladly give you my new shoes if you would take me to her palace. Your water goes everywhere, even in the winter. Since you were once ice, surely you must have seen the Snow Queen's palace." It seemed the waves nodded in a strange manner; so Gerta took off her wooden shoes, the most precious things she possessed, and threw them both into the river. She hopped into a boat that was on the shore and began to drift downstream.

Slowly the boat carried her down the winding river. Soon it arrived at a cottage. Through its gate walked an old woman who looked friendly. She had a large broad-brimmed hat, painted with splendid flowers. "Hello, little girl!" she greeted Gerta. "How nice of you to come visit me. Where did you come from?"

"The river brought me," Gerta replied. "Is this the Snow Queen's palace?"

"The Snow Queen?" The old woman laughed. "No, this is my home, come and see."

Gerta saw an amazing garden, filled with beautiful flowers of all kinds.

"Oh, what beautiful flowers!" Gerta exclaimed. "My friend and I plant flowers like these."

"You must tell me all about him after we rest and have some

lunch," the old woman told her. "You mustn't worry about your friend. Come and enjoy my beautiful garden. There's plenty of time to find Kai. You need some rest." The old woman led Gerta to a couch in a comfortable greenhouse.

"How did you know about my friend Kai?" Gerta asked.

"There, there," the old woman said. "A short little nap will help you forget about everything. Let every day you spend here seem like an hour and every week like a day. Forget about the Snow Queen."

Against her will, Gerta slept. The lady was not a bad person. She did a little magic sometimes—little selfish magic. She was led by the Snow Queen, who was able to control the journey that Gerta must make.

When Gerta awoke, she could not remember where she was or what she had been looking for. But she recognized the smell of roses in the air, which reminded her of her dear friend Kai.

"Now I remember," she said. "Kai! I have to get out of here." She rushed through the gates and discovered that already it was autumn. The sleeping spell had lasted all spring, all summer, and into fall. Time was running out for Gerta. The Snow Queen was regaining her strength as winter approached, and after the first storm of winter, Gerta knew that Kai would belong to the Snow Queen forever.

Gerta reached the ocean and asked it if it had seen her friend. As she sat by the water, a big black raven came up beside her and greeted her. "My name is Carrson," he said. "I noticed you sitting there and because it is late, I was worried. Are you all right?" he asked.

"Well," Gerta replied. "I've been looking for someone who has been gone a very long time. Maybe in your travels you have seen him? He is a young boy named Kai."

"I may have," the bird told her. "Why don't you follow me to the palace? There lives a boy who may be Kai. My friend Carranna knows the palace well. She will help us sneak inside to see if the boy is Kai."

"Thank you," Gerta said gratefully.

That evening, Gerta, Carrson, and Carranna crept into the palace garden. They made their way through the large rooms, sneaking around the guards, and finally came to a magnificent bedchamber. The room held two beds that resembled gold lilies. In one, Gerta saw a blond head peeking out from beneath the blankets. Her dear Kai!

"Kai," she whispered gently. "Wake up." But as the boy awoke and turned his face toward her, she sadly saw that he was not Kai.

In the other bed, the boy's sister, the princess, awoke as well.

"Who are you?" they asked in surprise. Little Gerta told the children about Kai and how she was searching for him everywhere. As Gerta told the prince and princess her story, Kai was falling deeper and deeper under the Snow Queen's spell.

In the Snow Queen's palace, Kai was looking intently at the ice crystals. "They are more perfect than any flower," he told the Snow Queen. "They are so exact. Not a single crooked line in any of the pieces."

"You are very clever, Kai," the Snow Queen responded.

"But they don't smell very sweet at all," Kai said.

"Kai, I have told you this before," the Snow Queen explained. "There are no smells or poet's songs. There is no joy or sad tales. You must forget all of this, Kai." She asked him if he could remember joy or beauty or love, and all he could remember was a faint glimmer of roses—and Gerta. "It's all right," said the Snow Queen. "Very soon your heart will be as hard as a diamond. These memories will not bother you again."

In the other warm palace, the good prince and the princess were helping Gerta with her search, giving her a golden carriage to speed her journey, good food, and warm clothes to protect her from the approaching winter storms. They called good-bye and wished her good luck in her journey.

Gerta swiftly rode through the dark night. But as the forest grew darker, the brilliant light of the beautiful carriage attracted the attention of a band of robbers. They followed the dazzling light until they rushed upon it.

"Oh, aren't you dressed in such fine clothes," the robbers exclaimed. "And a beautiful hat, little princess. I want that coat!" Just as the robber woman was about to take Gerta's coat from her, she was pounced on by a little robber girl.

"No," the little robber girl shouted. "She is my toy! Give that to me." She turned to Gerta. "They won't hurt you now . . . at least until I say so!" She took Gerta's mittens and hat from her and led her away to the cave where she lived. In her small room, the little robber girl kept forest animals tied up as her toys. She

kept white pigeons and small rabbits. She also had a large reindeer tethered to the wall. All of the animals were very frightened of the little robber girl. "Now you are my newest toy," she told Gerta, "a little spoiled princess."

"But I'm not a princess," Gerta told her. "I'm a simple girl, like you. I'm trying to rescue my best friend, Kai. He is at the Snow Queen's castle."

"Where?" the robber girl demanded. "Sit down. I want to know everything about it."

"Kai is the kindest boy that ever lived," Gerta told her. "One night during a terrible storm, the Snow Queen appeared to us.

She put a spell on Kai, and he became a different person. He became mean and cold, just like her. A few days later, she rode her sleigh into our town square. Kai was still under her spell and attached his sled to her sleigh. And then the sleigh vanished, taking Kai with her to the cold north."

"He's lucky to have a friend like you," the robber girl said. "We must do something!"

The girl's pigeons had overheard Gerta's story and spoke up. "We have seen him. Your friend Kai passed us. He was with the Snow Queen. She flew over our nest, up north in Lapland. Her breath froze everyone but us."

"Lapland?" Gerta said. "But where?"

"I am from Lapland," the reindeer said. "Oh, how beautiful and free it is there."

The robber girl thought about this and decided that she, too, could help Gerta.

"Look here," she said to the reindeer. "I'll let you go home, but with one condition: You must take this girl to the Snow Queen."

Gerta was very grateful. "You are a good friend to me and Kai," she told the girl. "You have a good heart."

The robber girl was sad to see her go. "I never had a friend," she said. "You're the only one who ever was kind to me." As she watched her new friend leave, the robber girl opened all the cages and freed the animals. For the first time in her life, tears rolled down her cheeks.

Gerta and the reindeer rode off toward Lapland. Soon the reindeer brought her to the little house of a Lapland woman.

"Oh, you poor things," the woman said when Gerta told her why she had come. "It's true. The Snow Queen was here, but it was long ago, and she never stopped her sleigh."

"Did you see Kai?" Gerta asked.

"Hmm." The woman tried to remember. "There was some-one. He was cold and sad. You must get to him before the first storm of winter ends. Here, take this note to my friend, the old Finnish woman. She will help you." She wrote a brief message on a frozen fish.

Gerta thanked the woman, and she and the reindeer set off for the Finnish woman's

home. Both Gerta and the reindeer were exhausted from their long and cold journey and lay down to rest. As the Finnish woman read the note, she said, "There is little time. The storm is fading, and soon Kai will belong to the Snow Queen. I know you are tired, but you are strong. What can be stronger than a loyal heart?"

Gerta immediately hopped on the reindeer and rushed out into the storm. She didn't even stop to put on her warm clothes or shoes. As he ran, the reindeer's strength began to leave him, and he could not carry Gerta the rest of the way. Gerta continued on alone. The Snow Queen sent her strongest winds and wildest blizzards to try to stop Gerta from reaching her palace.

But at last Gerta finally arrived and found Kai inside. "Kai," she called. "It's me! Gerta! Don't you remember me?"

Alas, the poor boy's heart was nearly ice. He felt nothing for his dear old friend. Gerta wept and embraced her friend, holding him tightly. Gerta's hot tears fell on his chest and penetrated into his heart. They thawed the lumps of ice and melted the splinters of the magic mirror that had caused him to forget his earlier life.

As his heart began to warm, Kai burst into tears. He wept so much that the icy splinter washed out of his eye, and he recognized his dearest friend. He began to feel the cold around him, but

Gerta warmed him with her love. As they rejoiced, the Snow Queen came upon them.

"The storm is over," Gerta said. "He's not yours. I was here before the end of the first winter storm. Leave us alone!"

"You are right," the Snow Queen told them. "I have no power against the warmth of two loving hearts." As she said this, the Snow Queen and her palace disappeared into the cold air, leaving the children alone together.

"We're free!" the children cried. "We're going home."

As the children passed those who had helped them, they called their thanks. They finally returned to their tiny rooftop garden and saw that the beautiful roses they had planted together had started to bloom, just for them. ✱

The Last Petal

Once upon a time there lived a girl named Jenny who loved to count. As she walked from one place to another, she would count nearly everything she saw. She would count the crows flying overhead and the lines on the sidewalk beneath her feet. One hot summer day as she was looking up to count every window she passed, she bumped into a bench. Sitting there was a boy about her age, reading a book.

"Hi," Jenny said in surprise. "Do you live around here?"

"Yes," the boy replied. "We moved here yesterday."

"What's your name?" Jenny asked, pleased to have a new playmate in the neighborhood.

"Victor," said the boy.

"And my name is Jenny, and I know how to count . . . and to read!" Jenny pointed to a store across the street. On the window there was a picture of a snake coiled around a shield. A man with a cane walked inside. "That's a pet store over there! Don't you see the snake?"

"That's not right." Victor laughed as the man walked out with new glasses. "That's where you get your eyes checked. Now the man can see!"

"Well, they should put glasses on the snake so people would know the difference!" Jenny sniffed. "You think you're so smart."

Next, Jenny went to the bagel shop to buy bagels for her family. The storekeeper strung the bagels on a long cord. As she walked home, she counted crows and did not notice that a stray dog was following behind her. Jenny finally felt a tug on the string and turned around to find the dog finishing off the last bagel.

"Oh, you bad dog!" Jenny shouted, and began to chase it. She ran and ran and soon found herself lost. She opened the gate of the nearest cottage, hoping to find someone who could help her find the dog. When she stepped inside the yard, Jenny saw an old woman standing next to a colorful little house.

"What do you want, little girl?" the lady asked her kindly. "What brings you here?"

"I am searching for a dog. I think he's around here someplace, and he stole my bagels!" Jenny replied. She heard a small noise and turned to find the thieving dog hiding behind the house. "There he is! That's the same dog!"

"Yes, he is my pet and he does like to eat bagels," the old lady told Jenny. "I don't have any bagels to give you, but I have something special." She pointed to a beautiful flower, each petal a different color. "As you can see, it's a very beautiful flower. It will make all your wishes come true. Just remove one petal at a time. Let it go and then say, 'Fly, fly away, my petal, through the east to the west, through the north to the south,' and then an enchanted magical circle will lift you into the air! When you have returned and touched the ground, you will have received your wish. You have seven wishes, dear, one for each petal."

Jenny kindly thanked the old lady, walked out of her garden through the gate, and only then remembered that she did not know how to get home. She wanted to go back to the little garden and ask the old lady for help, but the little garden and the old lady had simply vanished! In place of the colorful cottage stood a small playhouse and a sandbox. Jenny then remembered that she had a magical flower. It would help her get back home. She tore off the first petal of the flower and said, "Fly, fly away, my petal! Through the east to the west, through the north to the south. And when I land I'll receive my wish. Now, I want to go home and have my bagels!" No sooner had she said those words than she found herself lifting up and floating through the window of her house with a string of bagels in her hand!

"My goodness!" Jenny exclaimed. "This is truly an amazing flower. It deserves to be in my mother's best vase." Jenny was much smaller than her mother and had to stand on several chairs in order to reach the vase on the top shelf. As she was leaning toward the bookcase, a flock of crows landed on the windowsill, attracted by the bagels. Distracted by trying to count the crows, Jenny fell to the ground and the vase shattered into many pieces.

From the next room, Jenny's mother heard the sound and called, "Jenny, did you break something? What are you doing in there?"

"No, Mama. I didn't break anything, I'm just playing with my toys." Quickly, Jenny plucked off the next petal on her flower and whispered, "Fly, fly away my petal. Through the east to the west, through the north to the south. Now I'll make my wish. I wish to make Mama's vase brand-new again." As she finished her wish, a magical breeze swept into the room and collected all the pieces of the broken vase from the floor. They all fit back together again and the vase rested again on the shelf where it belonged. And just in time! Jenny's mother entered the room! Seeing nothing broken, she sent Jenny outside to play.

Jenny walked outside into the hot sun and, to her surprise, saw a small group of boys dressed in winter clothes, playing with a sled. She heard one of the older boys say, "Let's get the dog ready! Without our dog, it's impossible to reach the North Pole."

"Hello!" Jenny greeted them. "What are you doing in those clothes?"

"We're on an expedition to the North Pole!" the older boy replied.

"Oh, that sounds so exciting! Please, can you take me with you?" Jenny asked.

"No!" the older boy answered. "Girls can't come!"

"Fine," Jenny said to herself. "Who cares if they won't let me come with them?" As she began to walk away, she saw the boy she had met that morning sitting on the same bench. "Hi, Victor! Why aren't you getting ready for the North Pole?"

"Oh, I can't go," Victor told her.

"Well, you're no fun," Jenny said. "You just sit there all day. I will go to the North Pole myself, and you can bet I'll get there first!" She plucked a petal off her flower and whispered, "Fly, fly away, my petal. Fly through the east to the west, through the north to the south. And now I'll make my wish! I want to go directly to the North Pole!" No sooner had she said those words than a snowstorm appeared out of nowhere. She was whisked into the sky and landed, headfirst, in a snowdrift in the North Pole! As Jenny stood up and looked around, she quickly realized that she was not wearing the right clothing for the weather. She was dressed in summer clothes and the temperature was way below freezing!

She began to shiver in the cold and saw around her walruses

and polar bears, also shivering. "Oh, why did I want
to come here?" Jenny
asked herself. "I've never
been so miserable in my
life. It's just freezing!" As
she sniffled and cried, her
tears formed an icicle on

her nose. A pair of polar bear cubs felt sorry for her and
brought over a scarf and hat that had been on their snowman.

"How can you come here without any fur?" they asked
Jenny. "You must be freezing."

"Oh, thank you," Jenny said as she put on the warm clothes.
But she was ready to leave. She pulled a petal off of the magic
flower and said, "Fly, fly away, my petal. Through the east to
the west, through the north to the south. And now I'll make my
wish. Please take me home!" Immediately, she was whisked into
the sky and returned to where she had started. She landed next
to the group of boys, who looked at her in surprise.

"Where have you been?" the older boy asked.

"I have been to the North Pole." Jenny coughed. "And you
see, I caught a little cold. Two bear cubs gave me this hat and
scarf because it was impossibly cold!"

The boys laughed. "Ha!" said one. "If that is true, where is
your reindeer, Santa?"

Jenny was disappointed that they didn't believe her. She
walked back to the bench where Victor was sitting. "Victor, they
don't believe that I went to the North Pole," she told him.

"I do. I believe you," Victor said. "Was the North Pole extraordinary!"

"I could send them to the North Pole," Jenny told him as she put her hat on his head. "Forever!" Jenny stood up and walked toward the playground. When she reached the playground, she saw children playing with all kinds of toys. Some of the children had dolls and strollers, some had balls and jump ropes, some had tricycles and scooters. Jenny looked down at her flower, with just three petals left, and thought how much fun it would be to have all those toys.

"Fly, fly away, my petal. Through the east to the west, through the north to the south," Jenny said to the flower. "And now I'll make my wish. I want to have all the toys in the world!" As she said that, toys of all different kinds began to appear from everywhere and make their way toward Jenny. They fell from the sky and marched in on the street. They erupted out of every house in town. "Now you all belong just to me!" Jenny said with excitement as her parade of toys moved closer.

But the toys were moving in so close that Jenny could barely move! The dolls and animals called, "Mommy! Mommy!" All of the other toys joined in, calling, "Jenny! Jenny! Play with us! Play, play, play!" A toy train was whistling toward Jenny and chugging, "All aboard! All aboard for the Jenny train!"

"Oh my!" cried Jenny when she saw the commotion she had caused. "There's just too many of you! Please go away!" As the streets filled with toys, Jenny raced up to the roof of her building. From there, she saw toys still coming in from as far away as she could see. She would soon be buried in toys! The toys followed her up to the roof and were pushing her closer and closer to the edge of the building. Jenny pulled out her magic flower and said as quickly as she could, "Fly, fly away, my petal! Through the east to the west, through the north to the south. And now I'm going to make my wish. Please! Oh, please, make the toys go away!"

To Jenny's relief, the toys disappeared at once. "Well, that was just too much," she said. "All those toys were scary!" She looked down at her flower and saw that she had only one petal left. "I have one more wish," she said. "Now what will it be?" So Jenny got down from the roof and began to walk. She passed an ice cream stand and said, "I'm really hungry."

"Just imagine if I had all the ice cream!" But then Jenny pictured ice cream filling the streets and houses as the toys had done. "If I had just one ice cream, I honestly don't think I'd

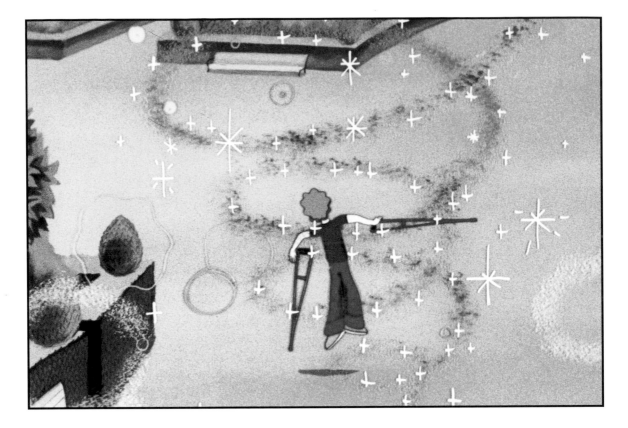

want any more," she admitted. "Maybe I don't want any ice cream." Jenny passed a lemonade stand.

"Just imagine if I had all the lemonade." But then Jenny imagined pink lemonade raining from the sky as the toys had done. "But what would be the point of a lemonade? I would wish for it and drink it, and nothing would be left."

Jenny continued to think and walk and soon came back to where Victor was sitting on the same bench reading his book. "Are you still reading?" Jenny asked him.

"Yes," he said shyly. "It's astronomy, about stars."

"Wouldn't you rather play?" she asked him.

"I would rather read," he replied.

"Oh, read and sit, sit and read!" Jenny complained. "All day long, like an old log!" Jenny snatched Victor's book from him and hopped around, teasing him.

"Give that back, that's mine!" Victor said.

"Well, I've got it now!" Jenny sang. "Catch me, catch me, if you can! Catch me, catch me, if you can!"

"You're just a spoiled girl," Victor said. He reached under the bench and pulled out a pair of crutches. Jenny watched in surprise as the boy stood with the support of the crutches and slowly walked away. She sat down on the bench. After a moment, she brought out her magic flower with one petal left.

"Fly, fly away, my petal. Through the east to the west, through the north to the south. My last wish is to make Victor healthy." She watched the air circle around Victor and lift him into the air. As his crutches fell to the ground, he slowly twirled around and landed gently. Jenny ran over to him and shouted, "Let's go play, Victor! You can walk! Now you can catch me!" Victor got to his feet and ran after Jenny. They chased each other back and forth, laughing all the while. Victor ran so fast that he caught her.

"Thank you, Jenny," he said. Jenny smiled at the happiness in Victor's eyes. She knew that with her last wish, she had finally gotten it right. ✽

Cinderella

Long ago, in a faraway kingdom, there lived the daughter of a forest keeper. She was as gentle as her heart was pure. Years after her mother died her father took a new wife, but unlike the girl's mother, her stepmother was selfish and cruel.

She made the poor girl work day and night for her and her spoiled daughters, Ormella and Asparagella. In spite of her stepmother's harsh treatment, Cinderella kept her unbounded patience and sweetness of temper.

One afternoon, Cinderella, her stepmother, and her stepsisters heard a proclamation from the palace. A messenger announced that His Majesty the king would be holding a glorious ball for his son, the prince. All the prominent ladies and gentlemen were invited to attend!

"A ball!" exclaimed Cinderella's stepmother. "Oh, daughters, what a wonderful and grand time we shall have."

Instead of permitting Cinderella to join her daughters in their excitement, the stepmother demanded that she get right to work sewing new dresses for them all.

On the night before the ball, Ormella, Asparagella, and their mother slept peacefully in their warm beds, dreaming about how glamorous they would look at the ball. Cinderella, however, worked all through the cold night sewing the gowns that they demanded. With a wistful heart, she dreamed about the good people who would be at the ball. She wished so much that she could join them in their happiness. As the solitary glow of the candle faded to sleep, so did Cinderella.

In the morning, Cinderella's stepsisters rushed to wake her so they could try on the dresses. As she watched them try on the beautiful gowns, Cinderella wanted so much to be able to go to the ball. That evening, Cinderella's father prepared to take his wife and stepdaughters to the ball. "Wife," he asked, "isn't Cinderella joining us?" The stepmother smiled at her husband as he left to prepare the carriage.

"Of course she is. Cinderella," she said, "I have good news for you. I've decided to let you go to the ball after all." Cinderella could not believe the good news! "Yes, you may attend after you wash the dishes, scour the pots and pans, sweep and polish all the floors, and scrub the fireplace until it is spotless. You must chop enough wood for one month, sweep all the dirt from the path, and water the roses until they all bloom. Wash all the clothes, including your father's old wretched undergarments. My darling daughters have been wanting new nightgowns for some time now; make them tonight. After you are finished you may come and watch the ball through the palace windows."

Cinderella watched them go with tears in her eyes. But she obeyed her stepmother and worked on her chores until she fell asleep, exhausted.

Soon she was awakened by the soothing voice of her fairy godmother.

"I'm here to help you, so shed not a tear," she told the girl. As Cinderella watched in amazement, her fairy godmother raised her magic wand. A pumpkin and field mice became a dazzling coach drawn by magnificent horses. Lizards became noble footmen to guide the way. The fairy godmother placed

her own sapphire crown on Cinderella's head as she transformed her rags into a radiant gown. Her final touch was a pair of crystal slippers that sparkled and glittered.

Delighted, Cinderella thanked her fairy godmother for her kindness.

As Cinderella hopped into the coach, her fairy godmother warned her to leave the ball by midnight. If she stayed beyond the stroke of twelve, her beautiful gown would return to rags, her coach would again be a pumpkin, and the horses and footmen would turn back into mice and lizards. Cinderella gave her fairy godmother her promise that she would leave the ball no later than midnight.

When she arrived at the ball, Cinderella, accustomed to keeping house, began doing so at the palace. The king was instantly taken by this kind and gentle maiden. As she watered flowers and straightened crooked pictures, Cinderella began to catch the eyes of all of the guests, who wondered where she had come from. Cinderella turned to see a handsome young man gazing at her. He could not take his eyes off the lovely girl. None were as impressed with Cinderella as the entranced prince.

The love-struck prince led Cinderella onto the ballroom floor to dance. As they drew together, they entered a world that belonged only to them.

All too soon, Cinderella heard the clock strike the first

chimes of midnight. She rushed away from the prince, barely bidding him good-bye. In her haste, she lost one of her crystal slippers. By the time the prince hurried outside, all that was left of his beautiful love was the tiny shoe.

The coachman raced as fast as he could to get Cinderella back before the last stroke of twelve, but it was too late. All the magic reversed, leaving Cinderella in her usual ragged dress, walking slowly home. The prince, the king, and all of the court tried to find Cinderella, but she had disappeared into the darkness of the night.

The next day, the palace messenger was sent to announce the prince's search for the owner of the crystal slipper.

"Hear ye, hear ye! By order of the king, all maidens are invited to try on this crystal slipper. She whose foot fits the slipper shall become the prince's bride!"

Cinderella's stepsisters and stepmother were very excited as they waited for the prince. When he finally arrived, Cinderella's stepsisters had quite a difficult time trying to fit the slipper onto their large ugly feet. Without thinking, her stepmother ordered Cinderella to help them. The prince instantly noticed her, and too late the stepmother saw her error. The prince had Cinderella sit, then raised the slipper. To everyone's amazement, it easily slid onto Cinderella's foot.

"I have found you," the prince said to Cinderella. "Will you be my bride?"

Of course she would. Cinderella was immediately taken to the palace, where she married her one true love. And in the many magical years that followed, the prince and his beautiful princess, Cinderella, lived happily ever after.

The Prince, the Swan, and the Czar Saltan

One cold night as shadows fell, the Czar Saltan rode through the land and came across a house where there lived three loyal maidens and an old woman who served as their guardian.

"Were the great czar to marry me," the czar overheard the first sister say, "alone, I would prepare a huge feast for all the world."

"Were the czar to marry me," said the second sister, "by myself, I would weave linen for all the people on the earth."

The youngest and fairest sister declared, "Were the czar to marry me, I'd ask only that I bear a son, a boy as mighty and honest and kind as he."

The moment that she had spoken these words, the door quietly opened and the Czar Saltan revealed himself. The words uttered by the third maiden had enchanted him.

"With deep respect, lady fair," he said, "come be my wife and bear this wondrous child of whom you speak. Come, good sisters. Won't you join us at the palace? Worthy positions will be found, I assure you, befitting your desires. Perhaps a royal cook and a royal seamstress. And as for you, old guardian, you may assist them."

They made their way the very next day to the palace to plan the wedding. The czar and the maiden were wed that very evening and all the kingdom feasted. But the two sisters and their guardian were so jealous of the new czarina that they wished her ill.

Not long after the czar was wed, he was called to lead his kingdom in a dangerous war. He promised his wife he would return swiftly, and told her to care well for their expected child. Months passed without the czar's return. Then, before the first autumn leaf fell, a healthy handsome baby was born to the queen. She named her prince Gvidon, and he was strong like his father and blessed with the eyes of his mother.

Putting quill to parchment, the queen wrote to her dear husband, telling him of the miracle that was their son. She entrusted her old guardian with safe delivery of the message. But this joyous message the king would never receive, for the

old woman had something quite different in mind. She and the two sisters replaced the queen's letter with one that told a more sinister message. This they passed to the scribe for delivery by horse.

Upon his arrival, the scribe read the message to the czar. "Revered sire, the queen gave birth last night and was struck with fear. She gave birth to neither son nor daughter, nor frog nor mouse, but to an unknown beast."

Though overcome with sorrow and anger, the czar instructed the scribe to return with a message for his wife. "My sweet wife, even though he may horrify, our child deserves our love."

Bearing this reply, the messenger returned to the kingdom. Arriving tired and hungry, he was easy prey for the three wicked women, who again replaced the intended letter. Instead of the czar's message of love, the people heard a decree commanding that the queen and her son, Gvidon, be sent to sea to die.

The czarina and her infant son were sealed up inside a barrel, which was then rolled down to the sea. Through the stormy night, the barrel floated on the sea. As he floated, the boy began to grow into a man, aging a year for every hour. His mother, however, did not age at all.

The czarina pleaded with the ocean to deliver them safely to dry land. The obedient waves gently pushed the barrel up onto a beach. The child, now a strong, grown man, gave a mighty heave and burst open the lid. Mother and son were safe from the sea, but found themselves on a tiny uninhabited island, home only to a few birds and a single oak tree.

Gvidon cut a branch from the tree and fashioned it into a bow and arrow—and just in time! He saw an ugly vulture swoop down toward a swan in the water. Just as the vulture was about to attack the vulnerable bird, Gvidon's arrow struck the beast. The vulture fell into the sea and the swan pecked at it viciously.

"You have saved my life, and I am indebted to you," said the swan. "It seems you are stranded on an island that is barren with no food and no fresh water. And what is a prince without a kingdom? Sleep now, and see what tomorrow brings."

When Gvidon and his mother awoke, they saw that the island was now a town with homes and towers, churches, palaces and golden domes. The czarina and her son had barely passed through the gates when they were greeted by the cheers of their new subjects who crowned him Prince

Gvidon, their ruler. "It seems the white swan is more than she seems," Gvidon said to his mother. All the townspeople cheered them, and with his mother's blessing, the prince took his throne and began his reign.

One clear day, the wind pushed a ship over the seas toward this newly built city. Excited by this kingdom that had suddenly grown on an island they knew as deserted, the sailors were anxious to add another stop to their trade route. The prince welcomed them and offered them food and drink. As they dined, the prince asked his guests, "Tell me something, gentlemen, of the world and its wonders."

One of the travelers replied, "Well, Your Grace, we have traveled all the world. We now know that the world is round, and Spaniards have discovered a new continent. I believe they called it America. And next we will travel past the Cape of Buyan to the kingdom of Saltan."

"May fair breezes speed you on," answered the prince. "And when you next see Czar Saltan, I pray, bow down low to him for me."

As the ship sailed off into the distance, Gvidon watched with melancholy as it neared the horizon. He saw his friend the white swan floating on the blue seas and spoke to her.

"Do you suppose the great Saltan ever thinks of us, dear swan?"

"Of course he does," replied the swan. "You never forget those closest to your heart. Perhaps, my prince, you should see for yourself."

Instantly, the prince became a mosquito. He struggled awkwardly with his new wings until he finally reached the ship's tall mast, which carried him past the Cape of Buyan to the kingdom of Saltan. Soon the coastline appeared on the horizon. At last, Gvidon would meet the great Saltan, his father.

The travelers went ashore, followed by the tiny bug, and were welcomed by the czar. But the czar was not at all what Gvidon expected. Was this the man who led great armies off to war? He seemed lost, even a little sad. Surrounded by his wife's sisters and their guardian, the czar invited the travelers to share with him the wonders they had seen.

"Your Highness, there is an island fifty leagues downstream," one of the travelers replied. "It was cheerless once, deserted and bare. Nothing but a tree grew on its banks. Then,

a gleaming city appeared, filled with joyous people, ruled by Prince Gvidon, who sends his greetings."

The czar was astounded to hear this, and wondered if the gracious prince was the same Gvidon whom he had lost. Should he pay a visit to the prince? But the sisters and their old guardian did not want Czar Saltan to leave.

"Cities, islands, contented peasants!" the sister cook exclaimed. "Why waste your time with that? Now I know a wonder that's worth telling. A clever little squirrel lives in a pine tree and cracks nuts all day long while singing. And not only that, each shell is of pure gold, and inside are nuts of emerald. Now that's a wonder, to be sure!" Hearing this, the czar was filled with amazement.

Enraged, the prince stung the cook in the eye, causing quite a commotion. He flew out the window to return to his island.

Soon after his return, the prince again spoke to the swan, describing the czar's awe in hearing of the magic squirrel. The prince also wished to see this marvel.

When the prince returned to his palace, he found an amazed crowd gathered in the courtyard. At the foot of a pine tree, a squirrel gnawed at a golden nut, extracting meat of emeralds. While he cracked the shells, the squirrel sang a song.

Astounded, Prince Gvidon whispered, "Thank you, swan."

The prince then built a house of crystal for the squirrel and kept it well guarded. A scribe recorded every shell, and the island's treasure grew.

Soon after, the good men of the sea journeyed again to Gvidon's island. Upon their arrival, the prince welcomed them and asked after Czar Saltan. When the travelers departed to deliver the unbelievable news of the squirrel to the czar, they carried with them one small but important passenger: a horsefly. The czar welcomed the travelers ashore and asked what they had seen.

"Do you remember we spoke of a wondrous city?" one of the travelers replied. "Grand and happy on a faraway island? Well, by the palace stands a crystal cage where dwells that very squirrel of which you spoke. All day long, the squirrel sings and cracks nuts of gold, extracting precious emeralds. Prince Gvidon reigns there. He bows to you."

"I would like to see this isle and visit this Gvidon," announced the astonished czar.

But the sisters and their guardian did not want Czar Saltan to leave.

"Truly, that is no miracle!" the sister seamstress sneered. "I remember being told that the sea would part and out of it would rise a legion of thirty-three giant handsome knights in gleaming armor, led by their uncle, the mighty Chernomer. Surely this is a greater wonder. Anything less is hardly worth traveling so far."

As the czar marveled over the words of the seamstress, the angry prince flew at his aunt and stung her in the eye.

Soon after, the prince

stood by the seashore and spoke with the swan, describing the newest marvel that the czar wished to see with his own eyes.

"I wish to see the thirty-three giant and handsome warriors in gleaming armor who rise out of the sea," said the prince.

Before his eyes, the sea rose up, then receded, and there emerged the thirty-three handsome warriors led by the white-haired Chernomer. As the prince looked on in amazement, the old man spoke to him.

"The swan, my niece, has sent us to you, sire, to protect your island and keep you safe from any harm that may befall you. My nephews, strong and able men, will gladly fight to protect your kingdom. We are here to serve you, Your Grace." Gvidon thanked them, and they returned to the sea.

It wasn't long before the news of this latest wonder reached the court of the czar. Again, Prince Gvidon had accompanied the travelers, this time in the form of a bumblebee. The travelers were welcomed by the czar and told him of what they had seen.

"We have seen the marvel of which you spoke," one of the travelers replied. "On an island, the sea parts and from it emerge thirty-three giant and handsome warriors led by their uncle. They are loyal only to Prince Gvidon and a small, graceful swan. The prince regrets your long delay and hopes you will soon visit."

"I would like to go to this fabulous island and pass a few days with Prince Gvidon," announced the astonished czar.

The sisters remained silent, but their old guardian spoke up. "A swan? A great fearless army loyal to a swan?" she said with contempt. "Perhaps it is time for your prince to put aside such childish pleasures and find himself a magical treasure. A princess! A beauty brighter than the sun who outshines the moon. In her hair, a crescent beams, and a star sparkles on her forehead. Many have tried to win her. Perhaps the prince could charm her heart away."

Seeing the czar marvel over what he had heard, Gvidon landed on the old woman's nose and angrily stung her. Chased out the window, the prince returned home to his island.

Soon after, Prince Gvidon again walked along the seashore and spoke with the swan, describing the marvel he had just heard. Upon hearing about the beautiful princess, the swan spoke to the prince. "That was not a vulture you killed, but a sorcerer. And I am not merely a swan, but your princess whom you seek."

The sea became tumultuous. A giant wave appeared and covered the swan as she ruffled her feathers. As the water calmed, she was transformed into the beautiful princess! A crescent

moon shone in her hair and a star sparkled on her forehead.

Gvidon and the swan princess married that very day, much like his father and mother had married long ago. The celebration continued for weeks, and soon the island was again visited by the travelers.

They took word back to the czar that the prince had married the very princess the old woman had spoken of, though this time they were not accompanied by a stinging insect.

"Forgive me, sire," one of the travelers said to the czar, "but I must speak. How often has Prince Gvidon sent his respects, bowed low, asked that you visit him? Indeed, if I may be so bold, sire, just what is the cause of your delay?"

"I lost a son named Gvidon," the czar explained. "To even say his name breaks my heart."

"If I may say so," the traveler continued, "this prince may not be your son, but he is every bit a man worthy of his noble name."

Hearing this, the czar could no longer delay his visit. He ordered his ship to prepare to sail, much to the displeasure of the sisters and their guardian.

"You made me a prisoner," the czar growled to them when they tried to hold him back. "Nothing but evil has come to me since I brought you here!"

Not long after, sitting at a window in his palace, Gvidon gazed out to sea and saw a fleet appear upon the blue horizon!

Through his spyglass, Prince Gvidon saw a royal fleet sail toward his happy island. "Mother!" he called. "Dear wife, come look! It is Father—the great Saltan!" In salute, cannons roared and bells sounded. The prince ran to the dock to welcome Czar Saltan.

The prince bowed to the czar, and the czar to the prince. Though the czar did not recognize his son, he was most impressed by the grandeur of the royal guard, the finely crafted palace, and of course the astonishing singing squirrel. As for the princess, the czar did not even notice her because by her side stood the czarina, his wife. The czar rejoiced with his long-lost but cherished family and was happy beyond belief. He even forgave the sisters and their old guardian, but banished them to a barren land where their lies would never be heard again.

The czar embraced his wife and toasted his son and his son's beautiful bride. They gathered Gvidon's subjects for a joyous feast, and all were happy for the rest of their days.

The Wild Swans

In a land far away there lived a king who had eleven sons and one daughter, named Eliza. As the children's good-hearted mother had died, leaving Eliza to tend to her brothers, the king chose a new wife to be mother to his children. Her name was Hildegard. The king did not know that Queen Hildegard was a wicked enchantress and did not love his children at all.

Soon after the wedding, early one morning before anyone else had risen, Queen Hildegard visited the eleven brothers as they slept in their beds. "You will be vultures by day, and human by night," she said, casting her first spell. Sure enough, as the first rays of the sun crept into the bedroom, the boys instantly turned to birds and flew up and out the window. But even the evil queen's magic could not destroy the goodness of the children. Instead of turning into dark, ugly vultures, the boys turned into beautiful and pure swans and flew into the air. "Hunt them!" shouted the queen to the guards, who immediately began to fire upon the poor swans. The swans circled the castle, hoping to see Eliza, but soon they had to flee for their lives.

Next the queen visited Eliza, fast asleep in her bed. The queen had brought three toads with her. To the first she said, "Seat your-self upon Eliza's head, that she may become as stupid as you are." To the next she said, "Place yourself on her forehead, that she may become as ugly and dirty as you are, and that her father may not know her." Then to the third she whispered, "Rest on her heart, so she will no longer be good and kind, but cold and selfish."

The frogs did as the queen bid, but when they had settled on Eliza, they instantly turned into beautiful roses and did her no harm. The princess was too good and too innocent for witchcraft to have any power over her. When the wicked queen saw this, she rubbed Eliza's face with a disgusting, smelly ointment that scarred her face till it was impossible to recognize her, and then darkened and tangled her beautiful blond hair with mud and twigs.

Then Queen Hildegard cast her final spell on the king. "You will not remember that you ever had any children," she declared. And it was so.

When Eliza's father saw her, he was much shocked by the girl's appearance. Of course he did not know her, and he ordered that she be cast from the castle and left in the forest. When night fell, Eliza laid herself down on soft moss and fell asleep.

All night long she dreamed of her brothers and their life in the castle. Everyone was happy. Then her father brought home his new queen, and Eliza, in her dream, saw what had happened to her eleven poor brothers. When she awoke, she began to cry, for however could she find them? An old lady suddenly appeared before her. Eliza did not know it, but the kindly woman was a guardian sent to protect her.

"Why do you cry, child?" the lady asked. Eliza told her the sad tale and asked if she had seen eleven swans.

"Indeed I have," the old woman said. "I saw eleven swans, each wearing a tiny golden crown, fly from the castle and head out to sea. Go to the shore and wait for them." Bidding the old lady good-bye, she headed toward the sea.

Many long years passed, and Eliza now lived by the sea in the hope of finding her brothers. One day, she spied a stag hurt by an arrow staggering toward a cliff's edge.

"Oh, let me help you," she cried. But before she could reach the wounded animal, the beast jumped off the cliff. Running to its edge, Eliza looked down and saw a miraculous thing. The stag had dived into a lake of clear water, and was emerging healed! The wound was gone.

As she looked in disbelief, a swan's feather fell at her feet. Looking up, she saw eleven white swans wearing tiny gold crowns!

"Brothers," she cried. "It is me, Eliza!" The swans landed nearby and one said, "You cannot be our sister. She was clean and beautiful, and you are so dirty."

Realizing she had to show her true self for them to recognize her, Eliza ran to the cliff's edge and jumped off. The surprised swans followed her, and saw to their amazement a very different young woman emerge from the waters. The scars on her face were gone and her hair was blond. At that moment, the sun set and the swans turned back into their human form.

Eliza uttered a loud cry, for although her brothers had aged over the years, she knew them immediately. She sprang into their arms. They laughed, and they wept, and very soon they understood how wicked their stepmother had acted to them all.

"We fly about as wild swans, so long as the sun is in the sky. But as soon as it sinks behind the hills, we recover our human shape,"

said the eldest brother. "Therefore we must always be near a resting place before sunset, for if we should be flying at that time, we would fall. We live in a land that lies beyond the ocean. It takes two days to cross, and there is a small island of rock where we can rest halfway. However can we take you with us? We cannot carry you, and we don't have a ship or boat."

"We can take her in a net," said another brother. "We can take turns carrying her." And so it was agreed. That night while her brothers slept, Eliza make a net of reeds and willows. Tired from her night's work, she laid down on it and fell asleep.

When the sun rose and her brothers again became wild swans, they took up the net in their beaks, and flew up to the clouds with the sleeping Eliza. They were far from land when she woke. They were now so high that a large ship beneath them looked like a white seagull skimming the waves. A great cloud floating behind them appeared like a vast mountain, and upon it Eliza saw her own shadow and those of the eleven swans, looking gigantic in size. It formed a more beautiful picture than she had ever seen, but as the sun rose higher and the clouds were left behind, the shadowy picture vanished away.

Onward the whole day they flew through the air like winged arrows, yet more slowly than usual, for they had their sister to carry.

Unbeknownst to them, Queen Hildegard knew of their plan.

She was delighted because it gave her the opportunity to drive them all into the sea and forever out of her life. She sent strong winds and cold rains to plague the swans. Their feathers grew heavy from the storm, and the net grew heavier still. The day was ending, and soon they would return to their human form. If they did not reach the island soon, they would fall into the sea!

Eliza watched the sinking sun with great anxiety. Suddenly the swans darted downward. Eliza trembled because she believed they were falling, but then she spied the tiny rock of an island. Just as the sun disappeared like the last spark of a fire, she felt her brothers' feet touch the rocky shore.

There was just room enough for them to sleep huddled together around a small, gnarled tree. No sooner had the last one closed his eyes then a crow appeared on the tree. Eliza did not know that this crow was in fact the old woman whom she had met in the woods.

"You wish to save your brothers," said the crow.

"Oh yes!" cried Eliza.

"Your brothers can be released from the spell," said the crow, "if you have courage and perseverance. Your brothers will take you to the cave where they live. Outside this cave grow stinging nettles. They grow there as well as among the graves in churchyards. These nettles you must gather even while they burn painful blisters on your hands. Break them into pieces with your hands and feet, and they will become flax, from which you must spin and weave eleven shirts. If you throw these shirts over the eleven swans, the spell will be broken. But, from the moment you commence your task until it is finished, even should it take years of your life, you must not speak. The first word you utter will pierce through the hearts of your brothers like a deadly dagger. Their lives hang upon your tongue. Remember all I have told you." So saying, the crow flew away.

At sunrise the brothers awoke and once again flew with Eliza high in the sky. Long before the sun went down, they came to the cave in the land that the brothers now called home. While they went in search of food, Eliza began her work with her delicate hands. She groped among the poisonous nettles, which burned great blisters on her hands and arms, but she was determined to bear it gladly if she could only release her dear brothers. Pulling up the nettles, she crushed them with her bare feet and spun the harsh flax they made.

At sunset her brothers returned and were very much frightened when they found she could not speak. But she appeared not to be harmed, so they became accustomed to her silence. By day her brothers would hunt for food and Eliza would work her nettles. Several coats were already finished and she was working on a new one the morning she heard the huntsman's horn. The sound came nearer and nearer, and she heard dogs barking, chasing a young bear that sought shelter in the cave. In a very few minutes, a group of huntsmen stood before the cave, and the handsomest of them was the king of the country. He advanced toward her, for he had never seen a lovelier maiden.

"How did you come here, my good woman?" he asked. But

Eliza shook her head. She dared not speak, at the cost of her brothers' lives.

"Come with me," the king said. "We cannot leave you here in the wilderness."

"It is best we did, sire," said the archbishop. He had hopes the young king would marry his daughter, and he wanted this beautiful maiden left alone. But the king ignored him and lifted Eliza onto his horse. She wept, but the king said, "I wish only for your happiness. A time will come when you will thank me for this." And then he galloped away over the mountains, holding her before him on this horse, and the hunters followed behind them.

As the sun went down, they approached a fair royal city with churches and cupolas. On arriving at the castle, the king led her into marble halls, where large fountains played and where the walls and the ceilings were covered with rich paintings. But she had no eyes for all these glorious sights; she could only mourn and weep. Patiently, she allowed the women to array her in royal robes, to weave pearls into her hair, and draw soft gloves over her blistered fingers.

As she stood before them all in her rich dress, she looked so

dazzlingly beautiful that the court bowed low in her presence. Then the king declared his intention of making her his bride, but the archbishop shook his head. He whispered that the fair young maiden was only a witch

who had blinded the king's eyes and bewitched his heart. But the king would not listen to this; he ordered the music to sound, the daintiest dishes to be served, and the loveliest maidens to dance. Afterward he led her through fragrant gardens and lofty halls, but not a smile appeared on her lips or sparkled in her eyes. She looked the very picture of grief. Then the king opened the door of a little chamber in which she was to sleep; it was adorned with rich green tapestry to resemble the cave in which he had found her. On the floor lay the bundle of cloth that she had spun from the nettles, and under the ceiling hung the shirts she had made. These things had been brought away from the cave as curiosities by one of the huntsmen.

"Here you can dream yourself back again in the old home in the cave," said the king. "Here is the work with which you employed yourself. It will amuse you now, in the midst of all this splendor, to think of that time."

When Eliza saw all these things that lay so near her heart, a smile played around her mouth. She thought of her brothers and their release, and this made her so joyful that she kissed the king's hand. She began to spend her days making the shirts that would free her brothers.

In the meantime, Queen Hildegard knew that the storm had not stopped Eliza and her brothers. She also knew of the intent of the archbishop to have his daughter wed the king. So Hildegard sent a knight to challenge the king. She made a charm for the knight so that he could never lose in battle. If the knight should win, then he would become king and wed the archbishop's daughter.

The day of the contest between the knight and the king was sunny and warm. Again and again the two men raced their horses toward each other, lances in hand. Finally, the black knight was knocked down. The king's love for the beautiful Eliza proved much too strong for Hildegard's sorcery. Again the queen's plans were thwarted.

That evening the archbishop had one of his men spy upon Eliza. He thought surely she would do something to raise suspicions of her being a witch. It was so unusual that she never spoke.

That night, Eliza continued to work on the eleven shirts. She had but one left to make, but she did not have enough nettles. She knew that the nettles she needed grew in the churchyard and that she must pluck them herself. How could she get out there? She decided to wait until everyone was asleep. Then she crept into the garden in the broad moonlight. She passed through the narrow walks and the deserted streets till she reached the churchyard. One person only had seen her, and that was the archbishop's spy.

The next day the archbishop told the king what had been seen. "She goes to the churchyard every night, Your Majesty, to consort with ghosts and evil spirits. She uses those nettles for evil spells. She is a witch!" But when the king pleaded with Eliza to speak up to defend herself, she said nothing. Believing that she did not

love him, the king saddled his horse and fled into the woods to hunt and think.

Alone, the archbishop told the people what he had seen and that Eliza was a witch. Angered by the story, the towns people cried out that Eliza must be burned at the stake at dawn. Eliza was led to a dark, dreary cell, where the wind whistled through the iron bars. Instead of soft covers to make her bed, her guards gave her instead the shirts she had woven and the bundle of nettles for a pillow. Nothing could have pleased her more. She continued her task with joy, and prayed for help, while not a soul comforted her with a kind word.

Toward evening, she heard at the grating the flutter of a swan's wings. It was her youngest brother. He had found his sister, and she sobbed for joy, although she knew that very likely this would be the last night of her life. He told her how they had all been searching for her. Soon he flew back to his brothers to tell what he had seen. As night fell, the brothers rushed back to the king's castle to save their sister. It was still night, and at least an hour before sunrise, when the eleven brothers stood at the castle gate and demanded to be brought before the king. They were denied, and so the princes tried to fight their way to their sister's prison cell.

The king, hunting in a nearby wood, heard the commotion and quickly returned to his castle. The town was now awake, and the people gathered to see Eliza punished. The archbishop placed the young woman on a cart and led her to the stake. She clutched the eleven shirts, all finished, and at last called to her brothers.

At that moment, the sun rose. The eleven brothers were seen no more, but eleven wild swans flew into the courtyard, followed by the king on horseback.

The eleven swans flew to Eliza. She hastily threw the eleven shirts into the air. As the swans flew into them, they immediately became eleven handsome princes. The spell was broken. Queen Hildegard lost her power.

"Now I may speak," Eliza exclaimed. "I am innocent." When he heard the entire story, the young king begged Eliza to become his queen. Of course Eliza agreed to marry him. That very day, a wedding was held in the castle, such as no one had ever seen before.

Ivan and His Magic Pony

Long ago in a small woodland village there lived an old man who had three sons. The oldest son had the brains of a donkey. The second son was as sharp as a worn-out tool. But it was the youngest son, Ivan, who earned the name Ivan the Fool. He was also rather short and plain. One night, their father sent them out to guard the fields. A thief had been lurking about and stealing hay. Ivan's cranky, lazy brothers were not pleased about having to keep watch at night.

"Ivan, you go and search all around from one end of the field to the other," the oldest brother told him.

"Yes, and we'll stay here to wait for the thief if he comes this way," agreed the middle brother, happy to rest.

Ivan took his place in the field and began to gaze into the skies to count all the twinkling stars. Soon he saw in the moonlight a mare as white as snow galloping across their fields of hay. Her mane and tail were golden, and curled almost to the ground.

Quietly Ivan approached her and jumped on her back. Together they raced over the fields and flew over mountains and forests. Though the mare bucked and kicked, Ivan held on to her long golden mane and dug in his heels. He would not let the mare throw him. As they flew, a dark storm grew around them and the mare became weary. Ivan filled his hat with rainwater and reached forward to offer it to her. "You must be thirsty," he said.

At last the mare stopped and spoke. "Kind lad, I failed to throw you, so now it seems you own me. But if you'll only let me go, upon you I will bestow two colts of stunning grace. They will be silken black with golden manes, and their hooves will be inlaid with pearl. These two will be grand enough for the czar's stables. And because your heart is pure and true, a third colt will be yours to keep. A magical pony with humps on his back and ears a yard long may look funny to you. But his worth is untold, and he will be your faithful friend for all of your days until the sun gets cold."

A gust of wind blew, and the three horses appeared. "How

wonderful they are!" thought Ivan. He agreed to release the magic mare, and led the two magnificent black horses and the humpbacked pony back to their small stable. He knew that the fields would be safe from then on.

Soon after, Ivan's brothers awoke and discovered the two colts hidden in the stable. They paid no attention to the lumpy little pony as they said to each other, "How could that little fool have gotten horses like these?"

The brothers set off with the black horses to see what price they would fetch at market. When Ivan returned to the barn, he found the fine horses missing and began to howl. "Oh, my beautiful colts with their golden manes, what wretch has stolen you away?"

The magic pony replied, "Two wretches, the ones you call brothers. Let's ride to town, master. Sit on my back and hold tight to my ears. And don't look down!"

They took off together with amazing speed. As they flew through the night, Ivan noticed a bright spot through the trees. It burned with marvelous intensity, but produced no heat or smoke. Ivan dug his heels into the magic pony and away they flew into the distance where the fire burned. The nearer they

flew to the fire, the brighter it burned, until an aura of light gleamed all around them.

"What wonder is this?" said Ivan.

"It is the firebird's feather," the little horse answered. "But beware, little master, its mischievous light is nothing to play with. Leave it behind, I beg you. Much sorrow and trouble follow everywhere it goes."

"I'll take good care of it," Ivan said as he picked up the feather, wrapped it in rags, and hid it in his hat. "Nothing will happen."

At last, Ivan caught up with his brothers and the two fine horses in the city square, where people came from all around to sell their goods. Ivan saw merchants offering the sweetest cakes, the ripest fruit, and bread that never went stale. Wonder! When the czar himself came riding into the marketplace, he saw the splendid creatures with their shiny coats and golden manes. He had to have them.

Ivan bargained with the czar for the sale of the horses—"Three scoops of silver!" said Ivan—and all he earned he gave to his brothers in spite of their dishonesty and deceit. Ivan truly had a generous and forgiving heart.

But as soon as the black horses were led to the czar's stables, they tore the reins from the groom and returned to Ivan. And so they did again and again.

"These colts will only behave for you," said the czar. "Therefore, Ivan, I hereby appoint you head of all stables."

"But Czar," said the groom, "am I not your stable master? Have I been cast aside for this boy?"

"You will be his assistant," said the czar. "Now go! And follow Ivan's orders."

So Ivan the Fool became the czar's stable master. He led the two beautiful colts to the czar's palace, and the little magic pony trotted along behind him, clapping his long ears together joyously.

The former stable master was not pleased to be a mere assistant, and hoped to ruin Ivan and regain his place as head of the
stables. He had noticed that every morning the black horses
were always clean and cared for, their troughs always filled with
fresh grain, yet Ivan never seemed to do any work. One night,
the jealous groom hid in the stable and kept watch over Ivan.

In the middle of the night, Ivan came in and took off his
cap. From inside his cap, he retrieved the firebird's feather,
which shone with brilliant light. Ivan set the feather in a bin
and began to groom the horses. He washed and brushed them
and braided their manes. He filled the troughs with food.
Finally, yawning, he wrapped the firebird's feather back in rags,
put his hat under his ear, and lay down to sleep.

Soon Ivan began to snore, and the assistant crept toward him,
put his hand inside the hat, snatched the feather, and was gone.

The czar was pleasantly dreaming when the assistant entered
his bedroom and roused him.

"Czar! Your Majesty," he sneered, "that boy, the new one, he's been keeping a secret from you. He's been hiding a fire-bird's feather! And what's more, the wicked fool claims that upon your order, he'll bring you the firebird itself. He's been boasting about it to everyone."

The czar blinked his eyes and marveled at the gleaming feather. Then he shouted, "What? But no one can catch a firebird! Bring that little boaster to me!"

When Ivan was brought before him, the czar shook the feather in his face and shouted, "So, my stable master, here I have shown you all kinds of generosity, and how is it you repay your czar? You hide a firebird's feather. I decree that if two days from now you have not captured a firebird and placed it here before me, alive at my feet, you will be hanged!"

When Ivan heard the czar's orders, he began to sob. He returned to the stable and told his troubles to the magic pony.

"You should have listened to what I told you," said the pony. "Much, much trouble does the feather bring. But I've got something in mind. Tomorrow we will manage this task."

In the morning, the little pony kicked up his heels and clapped his ears together. Upon the pony's bidding, Ivan prepared a basket of grain and honey. They flew over forests and hills, mountains and oceans, until they reached a quiet spot where the firebirds rested. Ivan set out the basket as he and his pony hid.

Soon the firebirds arrived, and the pony told Ivan to stay hidden while the birds enjoyed the sweet grain. Nearer and nearer to the boy the firebirds came. Ivan remained as still as he could. Then when a firebird was within reach, Ivan seized it and called to his pony.

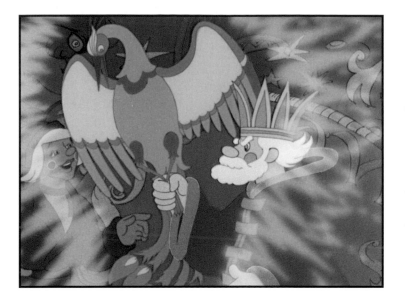

Instantly, the little horse was beside him. Ivan threw the firebird into his sack and hopped on the pony. Together they flew off like the wind, over forests and hills, mountains and oceans, until they returned to the czar's palace. Ivan marched into the royal bedroom with the firebird concealed in the sack and called, "I've got your firebird, Your Majesty!"

"Show it to me," demanded the czar.

"If you please, Czar," said Ivan. "First we have to be very, very careful. Close all the doors and windows so we are safely left in the dark."

When Ivan revealed the bird, such a light shone that all of the people in the castle covered their eyes, and the former stable master cried, "Fire! Put me out!" Ivan and the czar laughed at his foolishness. The czar named Ivan his commander of good advice as thanks for the marvelous gift.

The next day, the jealous assistant again came to the czar's bedroom, saying, "Czar, this time that Ivan of yours has been boasting of an even finer bird he'll catch for you. It's the mystical sea maiden whom you desire. He claims he can make her your bride."

The czar was very angry and had Ivan brought before him. "Hear me, Ivan, if by Christmas snow she is not brought to me, I'll have you drowned in the frozen river."

When Ivan heard this command, he again turned to his true

friend, the magic pony. "Please help me, pony. How will I ever find the sea maiden?"

"Don't worry, Ivan," said the pony. "I will lead you."

They set off together, flying for days, then weeks, until at last they reached the realm of the sea maiden.

On the shore by the sea, they set up a tent, hoping the sea maiden would stop to rest. They laid a luscious banquet to tempt her, and kept hidden until she arrived on a golden boat. After eating and drinking her fill of the fine food and drink, the beautiful maiden began to sing.

Her lovely singing enchanted the young Ivan, who had never seen nor heard such beauty. But the pony roused him out of his dreamy state, and together they captured the sea maiden as gently as they could. Away they flew over forests and hills, mountains and oceans, until they returned to the city of the czar.

Ivan was sad, because he had fallen in love with the sea maiden. He was not happy to be bringing her back for the czar to wed. Upon seeing his young bride-to-be, however, the czar began wedding preparations at once.

"But I am much too young for an old man like you," the sea maiden objected. "You are hunched and gray, and some of your teeth are missing. But there is a way to make old things new. Tomorrow at dawn, set three great cauldrons side by side in your courtyard. Fill one with ice-cold water, one with boiling water, and one with boiling milk. He who possesses a true heart and steps into these three baths will emerge a young and handsome man."

The czar did not much like the idea, but he ordered the three cauldrons filled. The jealous old stable master came to him and whispered, "Why not let Ivan jump into the pots first?" This sounded like good advice to the czar. But when Ivan heard the czar's command, he angrily refused and was thrown in a cell. Soon after he was visited by his faithful pony.

"It looks like the end of me, pony," said Ivan, weeping. "In the morning, the czar will force me to my death in the cauldrons of boiling milk and water!"

"It was the firebird's feather that caused your sorrow," said the magic pony. "But we will manage. In the morning, ask the czar to grant one last request: to see your little humpbacked friend one more time."

The jealous old stable master overheard these words and crept after the pony. When he was out of Ivan's sight, the man pounced on the pony, capturing him in a sack!

The next morning as the townspeople waited for Ivan to test the boiling cauldrons, he made his request to the czar and whistled for

his friend. The magic pony, strung up in a sack by the old stable master, heard Ivan's call and struggled to get free. Just as Ivan was about to be forced into the cauldrons by the guards, the pony freed himself and rushed to his side. He blew air onto each of the boiling cauldrons and then stopped at the edge of the ice-cold tub. Ivan leaped first into the milk, then the boiling water, and finally plunged into the freezing bath. The pony and townspeople waited with their breaths held until Ivan rose from the water, as handsome as a young man could be.

When the czar saw Ivan's transformation into a tall and handsome man, he jumped from his throne and raced toward the cauldrons. He dove into the pot of boiling milk, expecting that the baths would return him to his youthful, handsome appearance. But the czar never emerged from the scalding milk, for his heart was not pure and true.

The young sea maiden had fallen instantly in love with the handsome Ivan, and knew she had found a man with a good heart. So Ivan the Fool became Ivan the Czar, and he lived and ruled happily with his queen and his faithful magic pony.

Pinocchio and the Golden Key

One evening, Giuseppe the carpenter started carving a leg for a chair from a log. However, after the first cut he heard a noise that seemed to come from the log. He thought that he must be hearing things, but when he tried to carve from another spot, the log cried out again, as if in pain. He put the log down for he did not feel well. Just then, his old friend Papa Carlo the organ-grinder walked in.

Giuseppe, seeing that old Carlo was in need, offered him the log so that he might carve out a toy to put next to his organ. Papa Carlo went home and started making a puppet. When he was done, he was amazed, for the puppet, a wooden boy, could speak, run, and dance. It delighted Papa Carlo, for he did not have any children of his own. He called the living puppet Pinocchio.

Pinocchio was a mischievous boy who did not obey his father. He broke dishes and ran after mice, and he even poked his long nose right through Papa Carlo's lovely painting of a fire burning on a warm hearth.

Kindhearted Papa Carlo was at his wit's end. "Pinocchio, as long as you keep your long nose out of other people's business, you will be fine," he said to the puppet. "I know what will keep you busy!" And so he sent Pinocchio to school. Papa Carlo was very poor, but he exchanged his coat for an ABC book for Pinocchio. The next morning, he sent Pinocchio to school.

On his way there, Pinocchio heard a man calling, "Hurry, hurry! Come to Karabas's Happy Theater of Happy Puppets!" A puppet show! Pinocchio wanted to go to school to learn and make Papa Carlo proud, but he could not resist.

The show delighted Pinocchio. The actors in the play were wooden puppets just like him! The performers, led by a delicate and sad black-and-white puppet named Pierro, noticed Pinocchio in the audience and welcomed him onto the stage to sing and dance with them. While he was happily dancing with his new friends, Pinocchio was snatched up by the cruel Karabas, the fearsome master of the puppet troupe. "Your freedom days are over, boy," Karabas said, laughing. "You belong to me now!"

"Let me go!" squealed Pinocchio. "I belong to my Papa Carlo!" How he regretted not listening to the kind old man. Karabas brutally dragged Pinocchio into his quarters and hung him on a hook next to an old astrologer puppet. "Who are you?" asked the frightened wooden boy, after Karabas had left.

"I look like the good wizard from whose enchanted tree we are all carved," answered the astrologer.

"I never heard about him!" said Pinocchio. "Please tell me!"

The astrologer began his story. "Once there lived a good wizard who grew an enchanted tree. From its wood, he carved wondrous wooden people who came to life."

"That's us!" cried Pinocchio.

"Yes," said the astrologer, nodding. "But the greedy Karabas-Barabas stole all of the little people away and made us his slaves. Karabas also stole a key from the wizard, but he could not find its lock. All he knew was that the magical key would unlock a golden treasure hidden beyond a fire."

"What happened then?" asked Pinocchio.

"Karabas cannot keep his evil secrets. Once I have heard him say that, in time, the magical tree fell, and was cut into logs and sold away.

"And from that wood . . . Papa Carlo made me!" said Pinocchio, amazed. "I'd like to meet this wizard."

"Oh, alas, his golden soul vanished forever," said the old astrologer. "His only wish was that we would be happy and perform in freedom in the care of a person with a kind heart— and Karabas destroyed that wish by enslaving us all here in misery. Only our lovely sister Malvina was able to get away."

The astrologer fell silent. The evil Karabas had returned. "When I find that golden treasure, I'll burn all those pesky puppets!" Karabas grumbled to himself. "For now, though . . . this new puppet, Pinocchio, will make a fine piece of kindling for my fire." Karabas took Pinocchio from the hook and beckoned him to come closer to the fire to get warm.

Pinocchio drew back. "No, thank you, sir. I poked my nose into Papa Carlo's fireplace, and I didn't get warm. I just poked a hole in it!"

"But you can't poke a hole in a fireplace," Karabas roared, "even with *your* nose!"

"Of course you can," Pinocchio replied, "if the fireplace is only painted on a piece of canvas."

"A fire, you say?" All at once, Karabas realized that Papa Carlo's painted fireplace was the very one that hid the treasure! And Karabas had the golden key. Suddenly he became very friendly to Pinocchio.

"My dear friend!" Karabas said to Pinocchio. "Your Papa Carlo must miss you and your nose so. Take these golden coins to him. Off you go."

Delighted to be free once again, Pinocchio set off. Karabas watched him go. He had to get that treasure! But how?

That night on a bridge across a small pond, Karabas met

with Alicia the fox and Basilio the cat. "I have a job for you," he said. "Find Pinocchio and follow him." But as he was paying them with some coins, the magical key slipped from his pocket and fell into the pond below.

Walking home with coins from Karabas, Alicia and Basilio stopped Pinocchio.

"Oh! Aren't you Pinocchio?" they said. They dared not rob him in daylight on the open road. "I've heard that you are a brave and clever boy. How would you like to give your Papa Carlo ten times the amount of money that you have now?"

"Oh yes, yes!" said Pinocchio, never stopping to wonder how they knew his name.

"Travel to the Field of Wonders. There you must dig a deep hole in the field and three times say, 'Kreks, pheks, peks.' Put gold coins in the hole and sprinkle with salt. Then go to sleep. In the morning, a magnificent tree will have grown, bursting with golden coins! The Field of Wonders is right over there, beyond that forest."

Pinocchio thanked them and ran into the woods. Alicia and Basilio quickly disguised themselves as ghosts, then followed him.

In the woods, Pinocchio was making his way to the Field of Wonders when suddenly he was set upon by ghosts. "Help!" he cried. He tossed the coins into his mouth and ran with all his might deep into the woods. Spying a tiny cottage, he pounded on the door to be let in. But the cat and the fox, disguised as the robbers, caught him and strung him up by his feet, hoping that the coins would fall out of his mouth.

Pinocchio did not call for help so that the coins would stay in his mouth. At last Alicia and Basilio decided to wait until the morning. So they went away for the time being, muttering angrily at the delay.

Later that morning, inside the beautiful tiny cottage, the blue-haired Malvina was awakened by her trusty friend, the poodle Artemon. She stepped outside into the late-morning sun. "What's that?" she exclaimed, seeing Pinocchio hanging by his feet in a nearby tree. She brought him down from the tree. She invited him into her home and fed him. Learning he had no schooling, over the next few days she tried to teach him how to read and write.

But Pinocchio misbehaved and neglected his studies. Annoyed, Malvina locked him in the attic to give him time to think.

While Pinocchio was thinking, not too far away, Karabas discovered that he had lost his magic key. Furious, he asked his friend Durimar to retrace his steps and find the key at all costs. He was determined to find that treasure!

Pinocchio sat in the darkness of Malvina's attic. Suddenly, he heard a whistle. A bat hung by the window.

"I am here to bring you a message from Alicia the fox and Basilio the cat," the bat said. "They are desperately waiting to take you to the Field of Wonders." As the clock struck midnight, Pinocchio broke out through the window and followed the bat to the fox and cat. They led him to a dark field and told him that he had arrived at the Field of Wonders!

The fox and cat watched Pinocchio as he dug a hole and dropped in the coins. Then they waited for him to fall asleep so they could dig up the coins.

"He's not going to sleep!" moaned Basilio after a while. So while Pinocchio watched the hole, wide awake, the fox and cat found the police chief and convinced him that a small wooden boy was planning an assault on him.

"Outrageous!" gasped the police chief, and he ordered Pinocchio to be caught and thrown into the pond. The puppet was soon discovered in the field, and the chief sent his dogs to chase him. Alicia and Basilio finally had their opportunity to collect the coins that they had been chasing for so long.

Splash! Pinocchio was thrown into the pond. "Who are you?" said a group of friendly little frogs.

"Pinocchio," he said, and he told them his sad story of trying to bring coins home to his poor Papa Carlo.

"Oh, we have heard of your Papa Carlo! But old Tortella knows much more!" said the frogs in unison. "Tortella, wake up! Listen to this!"

Tortella the turtle paddled over and listened to Pinocchio tell his story all over again. Then she described to Pinocchio what she had seen and heard days before. She had been below the bridge when the golden key fell from Karabas's pocket!

"This is for you," said Tortella, giving Pinocchio the key. "My friend the old good wizard once said that this key will belong to the last puppet of his wonderful enchanted tree. Remember, it unlocks a great gift."

"But where?" said Pinocchio.

"Only the fat man with the black beard knows where the treasure lies," said Tortella.

"Thank you, Tortella," said Pinocchio. "You are a good friend."

Pinocchio took the key and ran off. Soon he came across his old friend Pierro. Pierro told him that things had been very bad at the theater because Karabas was so upset about losing the key.

"But I have the key!" Pinocchio said joyously. Together they ran to Malvina's house, who was very happy to see little Pinocchio and Pierro.

Suddenly, a frog jumped in. "Pinocchio!" he cried. "Durimar

caught Tortella and forced her to confess. Now Karabas knows you have the key. He's enraged, and he has vowed to hunt you down!"

"I hear him coming!" said Pinocchio. "Pierro, take Malvina to the pond, where it is safe." Pinocchio ran outside and quickly climbed a tree.

"Give me my key!" exclaimed Karabas, climbing up after him.

Pinocchio caught the end of the evil man's long beard, tied it to a branch, jumped off the tree, and ran around it in circles. Karabas chased Pinocchio, all the while getting more and more entangled in the tree. "Take that, you hairy bully," said Pinocchio—and suddenly Karabas was hanging from the tree by his black beard.

Pinocchio found his friends Pierro and Malvina and Artemon the poodle hiding in a cave. Karabas had freed himself, and now he was roaring and crying, promising to catch Pinocchio. With that thought he went to the tavern.

"Karabas is the fat man with the black beard! I must follow him and find out where the treasure is. Then we can all open it with the golden key!" said Pinocchio.

Pinocchio followed Karabas into a tavern. He hid in a jug—ugh! It was full of all kinds of bones! Still, no one could see him.

In his most frightening and haunting voice, Pinocchio called to Karabas from the echoing jug, "You, Karabas! Tell me where the door to the treasure is."

Karabas thought he was hearing the voice of a ghost and grew very frightened. "In Papa Carlo's room, behind the painted fireplace," he answered fearfully. As Karabas cowered, Alicia and Basilio entered the tavern. The police dogs had tracked Pinocchio's scent, and the fox and the cat knew that the puppet was hiding nearby.

"Mr. Karabas!" Alicia said loudly. "The police have captured Pinocchio's friends Pierro and Malvina." Pinocchio gasped in dismay and popped his head out of the jug. Basilio immediately spotted him and grabbed the container.

Alicia set the jug in front of Karabas. "And here is Pinocchio! Your little wooden prize!"

Pinocchio jumped out of the jug with a clatter of bones, scaring everyone for a second. He hopped onto the back of a kind rooster. "I must rescue my friends Pierro and Malvina," he said. The rooster hastily ran out of the tavern.

With the help of the rooster, Pinocchio managed to free his friends—but Karabas and the two robbers were right behind them! Just as they were about to be captured, Papa Carlo, who had been searching for his little wooden son, crept up the steep

hill and hooked Karabas's leg with his cane. Down Karabas fell into a big clumsy pile and rolled down the hill. Like all bullies, Karabas was a coward, so seeing himself outmatched, he collected himself and ran off while Papa Carlo hugged his little boy. And Pinocchio felt safe and happy in Papa Carlo's arms.

Pinocchio and his friends returned to Papa Carlo's house. Together, they removed the painting of the fireplace to reveal a hidden door. "Look! It's Pinocchio!" exclaimed Malvina in amazement. "It's Pinocchio carved on the door!"

Outside, Karabas was back—and he and his henchmen were trying to break down Papa Carlo's door. They could hear Karabas shouting in anger.

"Quick, try the key!" said Pierro. The boy fit the golden key into the door.

Just as Karabas burst in, the key turned in the lock! Papa Carlo, Pinocchio, and his friends ran through the tiny door and slammed it behind them. "No bully will ever get through my magic door," Pinocchio declared.

Inside, they followed a dark and winding stone staircase. Suddenly, before them they saw a marvelous sight! It was just the way the old astrologer puppet had described it to Pinocchio. It was the good wizard's magical theater for his puppets. Here at last was a stage, a great stage for the puppets to perform in happiness and freedom!

Together with Papa Carlo, the puppets opened the magical theater, where no one with bad intentions or a cruel nature could get in. All of Karabas's little actors ran away from him and came to Pinocchio's theater. Karabas came to the ticket booth only to find all the tickets sold out, and he became so angry that he lost his balance, slipped, and fell into a puddle on the street, where he sat until the final curtain that night.

The little magical troupe's first show was the fascinating adventures of Pinocchio and his friends. Kindhearted Papa Carlo directed the puppets in their songs and dances. It was to be the first of many, many performances, and Pinocchio, Papa Carlo, and the enchanted puppets lived in joy forever after, singing and dancing and bringing happiness to their thrilled and devoted audiences. 🐸

The Snow Girl

In a small village in a dense forest there lived an elderly couple whom everyone called lovingly and respectfully Grandmother and Grandfather, because they loved children with all their hearts. They lived in a warm log house and had plenty to eat because they had worked hard through the harvest. But as happy as they appeared to be, they always carried a sadness inside them, for they had no children of their own.

One cold day, Grandfather watched the village children build a

snowman. He decided he and his wife could make a snowperson
like the children did, and have a pretend child to soothe their kind
souls. That evening, he and Grandmother stepped outside into
the cold air and began to roll the snow and shape it into a little
girl. Before their astonished eyes, the figure began to move and
take on life. Overjoyed, they called their new daughter Dashinka.

Every day, the couple thanked the magic that had created
such a kind, helpful, and loving child. Dashinka helped them
with their chores around the house and loved to play outdoors.
She was always gentle and caring with the other children and
with animals. But Dashinka would never join Grandmother
and Grandfather by the warm fire in the cold evenings. Instead,

she would sit next to the window where the air was the chilliest. Though she could play and love like a real little girl, Dashinka knew that she was more delicate than the other children.

As time passed, everyone forgot that Dashinka was only made of snow and magic. When spring arrived, everyone was happy and spent as much time as possible outdoors in the sun. No one could understand why Dashinka was not as cheerful as they were, and why she chose to stay indoors.

Dashinka was unhappy because she could not play in the sun with the other children. She wished so strongly to be able to join them in their adventures. She watched them dancing through the hills, then gathering around a warm fire as the light faded. Though they urged her to join in their games, she knew that the heat of the sun and the fire would melt her frozen body. But how she longed to play with them!

One day, the children called to Dashinka as she sat by the window. They teased her to come and play a game of jumping over a small fire. She said she could not, but they urged her again and again. Dashinka so wanted to do as they did. Finally, she agreed and ventured outdoors. When it was her turn, she ran toward the flames. As she jumped over the fire, Dashinka, the child of snow, transformed into a beautiful cloud.

The other children watched in wonder as the cloud floated over the home of Grandmother and Grandfather. Then the cloud began to fall from the sky as a gentle soft rain. Where a drop landed, a beautiful white flower grew. Now the little snow girl found a way to always be outdoors under the sun, and also be with her parents, making them happy for the rest of their days. From that day, the other children in the village were more understanding of one another because they remembered the story of the gentle snow girl. ❄

Twelve Months

In a small, cold village, a wicked and selfish woman lived with her daughter and her stepdaughter, Christina. She loved her own daughter, but Christina could do nothing to satisfy her. Everything she did was wrong.

The daughter would spend the day lying about the warm house, eating sweets, while Christina did all the chores. She had to fetch water, collect firewood from the forest, wash the clothes, and care for the garden. Because she was always working outdoors, Christina grew accustomed to the bitter cold of the winter, the heat of the summer, the rains of spring, and the winds of autumn.

One cold December day as Christina was walking through the snowy forest, gathering firewood, she was quite surprised to see the forest animals playing games together and to hear them speaking to one another! She giggled as they raced beneath the snowy branches, playing tag. An old soldier was also passing through the forest and heard her laugh.

"How nice to hear laughter when everyone complains about the cold," he called to Christina. "What makes you so giddy, my little friend? Buried treasure, or good news?"

"Oh no," Christina replied. "I can hardly believe it. The animals are talking, almost as if they were human. It must be a miracle!"

"It is a day for miracles," the soldier told the girl. "Today is the last day of the old year. Tomorrow a new year begins, and today, until midnight, all the animals can speak in human voices. Today is a special day, where everyone should examine the past year and take a good look to see how they can become a better person. Do you think you could become a better person?"

"I suppose I could be, but I always try to be good," Christina replied.

"Trying is very important," the soldier said. "Sometimes you can get help from some very unusual places. My great-grandfather once told me that when his great-grandfather was a child, he met twelve brothers in these very woods. They would meet every new year's eve and select a kindhearted person to watch over for the new year."

Christina asked, "Do you think I will ever see them?"

"You never know," the soldier said. "For good people, anything is possible. Now why are you out in the cold with your sled?"

"My stepmother always sends me for the firewood. Otherwise we would freeze," Christina told the soldier. When he heard that, the soldier suggested that they help each other with their chores. He would help her gather firewood if Christina would help him find the perfect new year's tree for the queen. He explained that the young queen, who was hardly more than a little girl, had been very unhappy since her parents died, and was quick to punish anyone who did something against her wishes. For that reason, the soldier had to find her a very special tree.

"So the queen is an orphan, like I am," said Christina as she set about gathering firewood for her stepmother and stepsister, keeping her eyes open for a beautiful tree for the soldier. Working together made the time in the cold forest much more enjoyable. Soon they had found the perfect tree and gathered firewood, and bidding each other farewell, they returned to their homes.

Meanwhile, the young queen was taking her lessons. She lived in a splendid castle and had many servants who tried as hard as they could to find things to make her happy. Unfortunately, she had a quick temper and was very unreasonable. She would become angry at her kind and patient professor when she answered a math or spelling problem incorrectly. She thought that because she was queen, she could make two plus two equal five! When she became too impatient to continue her lessons, she demanded that her professor tell her stories instead.

The same day that Christina met the soldier in the forest, the queen asked her professor for a story about the new year and what it would bring. The professor told her about the twelve months and the four seasons: winter, spring, summer, and fall. "Each month brings us its own gifts," he explained to the queen. "The winter brings us ice-skating. In March, the air becomes warmer. By April, the first snowdrop flowers bloom from under the melting snow. And by May, we are fully into spring."

"Snowdrop flowers," the queen repeated, thinking about the pretty petals and warm weather. "I want spring now. I command spring to start tomorrow!"

"But that is simply impossible, Your Majesty," the professor

told her. "It can't be done! It is winter now, and spring simply cannot arrive until after winter finishes. It is the law of nature."

"Well, I will write a new law!" the queen exclaimed. "I will decide when spring comes!" So the queen gave orders throughout the land that winter had ended and spring had arrived. She commanded that a basket of snowdrops be gathered as a sign of the new order. As a reward, she would send the basket back filled with gold. But those who ignored her decree that spring had come and did not go out in search of flowers would lose their heads!

The stepmother and her daughter were at the market near the castle gates and soon heard the announcement. When Christina brought the wood home, they did not even give her a piece of bread or a minute to get warm before they sent her back to the woods to look for flowers. The girl looked at her stepmother in astonishment. She had just returned from the woods and the ground was covered in many feet of snow. There would be no flowers until April, no matter how long she searched! Sadly, Christina went back out into the cold forest. The windblown snow stung her eyes. She was barely able to move through the deep drifts. The forest had grown very dark, and Christina was frightened by the howling of a hungry wolf. Climbing to the top of a tree, she saw a glimmer of light flickering far away. She cautiously climbed down and headed toward the light.

As Christina neared, the light shone more and more

brightly. She could smell the warmth of the smoke in the air, and she could hear the crackling of the wood. The little girl hastened her step and emerged into a clearing. A big bonfire was burning in the middle, and surrounding the fire were twelve men of different ages.

Christina stared at them in amazement, wondering who they were. Since she was a small child, she had spent many days and nights in these woods, yet never before had she seen this gathering. All the men were beautifully dressed in fine robes and warm cloaks. Suddenly, the tallest and oldest man noticed the young girl who had joined the circle around the fire. He asked, not unkindly, "Who are you? Where are you from?"

"I only wanted to get warm," Christina replied. "I didn't mean to disturb you."

"Oh, please join us," the old man said, "but tell me, what is the basket for?"

The girl looked down at her empty basket and said, "I need to find snowdrops. If I do not return with a full basket, I will be killed!"

"Well then, you are in some trouble, little one," the old man said. "And I should know, for I am the eldest, Brother January. We are in the depths of winter. Snowdrops will not appear until April."

Christina sadly turned to go and continue her search, but one of the younger men—Brother April, she later learned—called after her. "Wait a minute! Brother January, perhaps I could borrow an hour of your time." Brother January agreed, and with the help of Brothers February and March, Brother April ruled for one hour. As Christina watched in astonishment, the snow melted and sun warmed the earth. The sound of birds chirping filled the air and small white flowers began to bloom.

"How can this be possible?" Christina said. "Oh, thank you, thank you, kind gentlemen." She began to fill her basket with snowdrops. While she collected her flowers, Brother January spoke to the eleven men.

"I know this girl. I have watched her as each of us passed by. She enjoys every month as it should be. She never complains in the winter cold, no matter how bitter. She is joyful and playful, and respects every creature and object of nature." His brothers agreed. They, too, had seen her fishing in the creek in June and tending the garden in July.

Christina returned to the circle with a full basket. "Thank you so much for the beautiful flowers," she said to them. "I have never in my life been treated with such kindness."

Brother April was so moved by her gratitude that he said to her, "Take this ring. I have chosen you to watch over for the year. If you ever have trouble again, throw this ring to the ground. Command it to roll, and we will all be there to come to your rescue, bringing all the powers of the twelve months. This is my promise to you."

"But you must never show anyone the way here," Brother January cautioned. "The path is secret except for a special few."

"I promise," Christina called as she hurried home. "Thank you, I will always remember your kindness."

She ran so swiftly, she could not even feel her legs beneath her. As she ran, spring gradually returned to winter. The moment that she reached her house, the winter wind howled and the forest grew dark. Christina's stepmother and step-daughter were amazed to see the girl return home with a basket full of snowdrops. Tomorrow they would take the basket to the queen to exchange the flowers for gold!

Early the next morning, the grumpy young queen was very disappointed that she had not yet received a basket of snowdrops. Even though the calendar showed that it was the first day of the new year, the queen disagreeably declared that the day was, instead, December 32. Her professor tried

to explain to her that she could not rewrite the calendar year, but the queen refused to listen.

"Today is December 32," she insisted. "And the day after that will be December 33, and so on. And every day in December, someone in this court will lose his or her head! And I decree that December will not end until someone brings me a basket full of snowdrops!" Just as she was ordering the preparations for the executions, Christina's stepmother and stepsister arrived in the queen's chambers to present her with the basket of snowdrops. Instantly, the queen's mood changed. She declared that the new year had begun.

As their basket was being filled with gold, the stepmother and stepdaughter made up a story about how they had found the flowers on the banks of a beautiful lake. When she heard this, the queen ordered her coachman to prepare a carriage to take her to the flowers. The deceitful mother and daughter realized they were trapped in a lie and admitted that it had been Christina who gathered the snowdrops.

"Well, then," the queen said, "I want Christina to show me the place. And if you want to keep your heads, you will not disappoint me."

The stepmother and her daughter ran outside to where Christina was waiting. "Christina," they said, "you must help us. Our lives are in danger! You must take us to where you found the snowdrops."

Christina would not break her promise to the month brothers, but she agreed to go in search of more flowers. The stepmother and her daughter ran back to the queen and told her that Christina would not lead them to the flowers. "But I have an idea," the stepmother told the queen. "Christina can go ahead by herself, but my daughter will follow her on foot. And we will follow my daughter in the royal sled." The queen agreed to this, and they set out into the cold, snowy forest after Christina.

Christina retraced the steps she had taken the day before but soon heard her clumsy stepsister following behind her. "Stepsister!" she exclaimed. "I should have known not to trust you. I won't go any farther. We're going home!"

"It's too late." Her stepsister laughed. "The queen herself is following in her royal sled. And you can't disobey the queen!" And just as she said that, the sled appeared through the trees.

When the queen saw Christina, she got down from the sled and brought her warm coat over to the freezing girl. "Why don't you want to give me more flowers? I can give you anything you wish and you can choose your reward. Show me where the snowdrops grow."

"Forgive me, Your Majesty," Christina replied, "but I can't do what you ask of me. I made a promise."

The queen giggled. "I don't ask for anything, I order! I order you to take us to the flowers!" Christina shook her head. She couldn't break her promise to the month brothers. In anger, the queen grabbed her warm clothes back from Christina. As she did, the ring that Brother April had given to Christina flew into the air and landed on the ground. "What a beautiful ring," the queen exclaimed. "Where did you get it?" When Christina refused to tell her, the queen grew angrier and bent to pick up the ring. "Fine!" she shouted. "If you won't tell me, then you can say good-bye to your precious ring." But Christina called out, "Roll, ring, roll!" as Brother April had instructed her. And as it rolled, she ran after it as quickly as she could.

The queen called to her guards to catch Christina. But before anyone could move, a gust of snowy wind blew by the Queen, her court, and the guards, chilling them to their bones. Then, to their amazement, they noticed that the snow had begun to melt and drip from the trees. Patches of green grass and flowers were emerging on the earth. "It's spring!" the queen exclaimed. "Listen! The birds are singing, and the snow is melting away!"

At an unimaginable speed, flowers were blooming! Strawberries were growing and the air grew warmer and warmer. After the powerful heat came a strong autumn rainstorm. The seasons were changing from spring to summer to fall and back to winter all within a few minutes!

"I want to go home!" whined the queen. All of the commotion was quite distressing to her.

"But we only have a sled," her chancellor told her. "And there is no more snow!" Just as he said that, it began to snow again. The seasons had returned to winter.

"Finally something that makes sense!" the queen's professor exclaimed. "It is January. Yes, it should be snowing in January."

Now the queen was cold. She saw a tall old man emerge and said, "You! Old man! I command you to get us out of here. I'll give you anything you want! I have gold and silver and . . ."

"I don't need anything from you," said Brother January. "I have more riches than anyone. My gold is in the beauty around me. Tell me, little one," he said to the unhappy queen, "what is your wish for the new year?"

The queen was so cold and worn out that she could not come up with an unreasonable demand and instead told the truth. "I am so lonely. I want a friend," she admitted, "a real friend."

"I understand," Brother January assured her.

The professor spoke up. "I would like for everything to be normal again. Everything in its proper time. Winter in winter, summer in summer, fall and spring where they belong. And me in my warm room with a good book . . . ."

"I want a coat!" the stepdaughter interrupted rudely. "I'm freezing! I would even take a dog fur coat!"

Upon hearing that, Brother January tossed two coats to the stepmother and her daughter. "Take these coats. They are yours forever."

"Dog coats!" exclaimed the stepmother. "You stupid girl, you should have asked for sable or mink!"

"This dog coat fits your face!" the daughter replied spitefully. "You look like a dog!"

The selfish stepmother and daughter argued until they began barking. Soon they turned into quarreling dogs. When the young queen saw that, she promised her professor that she would be well behaved and respectful from then on.

Brother January harnessed the dogs to a sled and rode back to his brothers and the bonfire with the queen and her attendants. When he arrived, he found that Christina had joined the brothers and was content in a warm fur coat by the fire. She greeted the queen and offered her a seat by the fire. When she saw the harnessed dogs, she said, "How odd. I've never seen those dogs before, but I know their voices. It's as if they are not barking but arguing."

"You do know them," Brother January replied. "They have not been dogs very long, but they have acted like dogs for quite some time. It is your stepmother and stepsister."

"Will they always be like this?" Christina gasped. "As dogs, I mean."

"They will live with you for three years as your guard dogs," January told her. "And after those years, if they learn how to

behave properly, we will remove their dog skins. Now, dear little one, it's time for you to go back. The blizzard will cover the path soon."

The month brothers prepared a beautiful sled, covered in silver bells and led by strong and graceful horses. When she saw it, the queen demanded that Christina give her a ride. In exchange, she would make Christina a member of her court. But Christina refused. "I could never tell you the truth, Your Majesty," Christina told the young queen. "If I disagreed with you, I might lose my head. I would not be happy like that."

"You must learn manners befitting a queen," Brother February told the young ruler. "If you ask nicely, you might be surprised at the answer. Perhaps you could speak more like a person, instead of a queen. Christina is a very nice girl. She could be your friend."

"I did ask for a friend," the queen said softly. "Excuse me, Christina. May I have a ride with you? I'm very cold."

"Of course I'll give you a ride," Christina replied kindly. "I'll even give you a fur coat that I won't take back. Because friends always take care of each other." She helped the queen into the sled and turned to the month brothers. "Thank you, my brothers. I will always remember your warm new year's fire!"

"And I will try in this new year to be a kinder and better person," the queen promised. "I hope to learn how from my good friend, Christina." As the queen and Christina rode off together, the brothers called new year's greetings to them. Through her kindness and generosity, Christina had shared the wisdom of the twelve months with her new friend.

Moscow's Soyuzmultfilm Studio

*O*ne of the best-kept secrets of the Cold War, through most of the past sixty years, was that the Soviet Union had an animation industry second only to the United States in quantity and quality.

At the beginning of the twentieth century, animation was in its infancy. The first Russian animator, Vladislav Starevich, began to animate insects in 1912 with a stop-motion camera borrowed from the Khanjankov Feature Film Studio. An entomologist by profession, he reportedly used actual (dead) bugs in his first animated short film, *The Beauty Lukanida,* and then switched to handmade large-scale insect models that were more flexible. Starevich produced approximately twenty delightful shorts about insects before emigrating to France after the Russian Revolution of 1917. There he continued to make animated films, segueing from bugs to horror and finally to films for children.

Following Starevich's departure, work in animation slowed and did not immediately resurface until the years following the revolution. Vladimir Lenin, the leader of the newly formed U.S.S.R., designated animation as "one of the most powerful media" for winning the hearts and minds of the largely illiterate Soviet masses. The very first Soviet animated film, *Soviet Toys,* a ten-minute short, was produced by the State Film Committee in 1924 as a "political advertisement." The film was directed by the innovative documentary director Dziga Vertov (*Kino Eye, Man with a Movie Camera*).

Soviet Toys was a frontal attack on NEP-men—Soviet capitalists who defied communism and became rich during the three years when Lenin tried to kick start the young state's moribund economy with his New Economic Politic (NEP). Using two-dimensional movable cutouts, which were the hallmark of early Soviet animation, Vertov animated a corpulent capitalist NEP-man and his lascivious lady friend indulging in decadent pleasures—until interrupted by a Noble Worker and a Peasant Farmer who unite to squeeze taxes from the NEP-man, thus defeating capitalism.

Dozens of anticapitalist and anti-American animated propaganda films followed, produced by enthusiastic film cooperatives. The movies were shown throughout the Soviet Union as shorts before feature films. For the next sixty years, animated propaganda films would continue to deliver the state's political messages in a clear and entertaining manner.

In the early 1930s, animators began to experiment with films for entertainment. At that time, too, sound and color were introduced. In 1933, a Walt Disney festival organized in Moscow so captivated Joseph Stalin, now the leader of the U.S.S.R. following Lenin's death, that the cutout technique was discarded in favor of cell animation, and the main focus of the Soviet animation industry became producing gentle, moral, nonviolent entertainment for children.

On June 10, 1935, a state order established Soyuzmultfilm as the U.S.S.R.'s first all-animation studio. A year later, Soyuzmultfilm Studio opened its doors in a building appropriated from the Russian Orthodox Church. The studio quickly became the main producer of animated films and the home of the most talented Soviet animation artists.

The studio's original mandate was to create animated films based on Russian and European fairy tales and folklore, classical as well as contemporary. The look was uniquely Russian, but the animation techniques developed by Walt Disney and others in Hollywood set the quality standards for art. Not until the 1960s did the American genre of "cartoons" with recurring characters in the style of Mickey Mouse and Bugs Bunny find an important place at the studio. And even then, "I'll Get You," Soyuzmultfilm's most popular cartoon series, was limited to eighteen ten-minute episodes.

The studio attracted some of the country's finest artists. Under communist rule, brushes, paints, and canvas were available only to "official artists," who were often required to create ideologically correct portraits of Soviet life and its leaders. Many who wanted more artistic freedom found their way to Soyuzmultfilm, where they used their art to create children's films with some of the country's leading writers and composers.

The profound quality of their art, together with the aesthetics of their animation, established Soyuzmultfilm as one of the great studios of

Europe. Many of the earliest animators, including Ivan Ivanov-Vano, the sisters Zinaida and Valentina Brumberg, and Leonid Amalrik, smoothly made the transition from animating propaganda to animating fairy tales.

Following the Nazi invasion of the U.S.S.R. in 1941, the staff of Soyuzmultfilm switched gears and began to make patriotic animated short films with titles such as *Fascist Boots on Our Homeland* and *Vultures*, many of which did not survive the war. These shorts were shown in cinemas across the embattled nation. Soyuzmultfilm artists also designed some of the striking graphic posters that appeared on walls throughout the U.S.S.R. to inspire and raise public morale.

Shortly after the war began, those artists not mobilized into the Red Army were evacuated to Samarkand, a desert city in the Asian republic of Uzbekistan. Work continued, but many major projects were put on hold and completed only after the war.

In 1946, *Song of Happiness*, a twenty-minute short directed by Mstislav Pashenko, won an honorable mention at the Venice Film Festival. It was the first Soviet animated film ever allowed by Stalin to be entered in an international competition. The following year, Soyuzmultfilm's first full-length animated film, *The Humpback Horse*, directed by Ivanov-Vano, was produced and caused a critical sensation when shown in the U.S.S.R. Abroad, it won the Marianski Lazni International Festival in Czechoslovakia. The 1975 remake (digitally restored in 1996 as *Ivan and His Magic Pony*) was honored by animation festivals from Bulgaria to Iran.

All of the films included in the "Mikhail Baryshnikov's Stories From My Childhood" series and gathered here in book form were produced by Soyuzmultfilm between 1952 and 1984. All were hand-drawn and shot on 35mm film for exhibition in movie houses. The earliest were rotoscoped (animated over the filmed movements of actors). Although consideration was given to production time and budget, Soyuzmultfilm's talented staff always had more artistic leeway than their commercially driven Western counterparts. Instead of adhering to an established style, the Soyuzmultfilm artists used their own unique artistry to animate the films.

For Soviet (now Russian) children, these animated classics are as beloved as Disney's *Snow White* or *Pinocchio*. Entertaining, nonviolent, imbued with good moral values, they nurtured generations of children, including series executive producers Mikhail Baryshnikov and Oleg Vidov. According to studio folklore, in the 1950s, Pope John Paul XXIII declared that "the best films for children are Soviet animated films."

After Stalin died in 1953, Nikita Khruschev became general secretary of the U.S.S.R. and ushered in a period of economic and intellectual liberalism from 1957–1964 known as the Khruschev Spring. Stalin and his crimes against the Soviet people were exposed at the 20th Party Congress, signaling to the Soviet people that the country would take a new direction after thirty-five years of fear and paranoia. The film industry began to explore new material and renewed styles of presentation.

In 1963, in his first foray as a director, Fyodor Khitruk abandoned the Disneyesque style that had dominated the films produced by Soyuzmultfilm from 1936. Returning to the early cutout traditions of the 1920s and early 1930s, he delighted audiences by venturing into the new world of civil reality with his groundbreaking ten-minute short *History of One Crime*. The new trend took hold and dozens of animators at Soyuzmultfilm and around the U.S.S.R. concentrated for the first time on the adult audience.

By 1992 Soyuzmultfilm had created more than twelve hundred films for children and adults. Each one was unique, artistically and intellectually crafted like an exquisite piece of Faberge.

With the advent of perestroika and economic reform, the studio found new patrons in the West. Teaming with S4C, a television station in Wales, in 1991, it coproduced the Emmy Award-winning miniseries "Shakespeare: The Animated Tales." Although many directors and artists left the studio to work for themselves or studios in Europe and Hollywood, masters such as Khitruk, Yuri Norstein, and Eduard Nazarov continued to educate new generations of animators in Russia. One of their prize students, Alexander Petrov, went on to direct and animate on glass the acclaimed *The Old Man and the Sea*, becoming the first Russian to win an Oscar (Best Animated Short Film of 1999).

In 1992, our company, Films by Jove, acquired distribution rights to much of the Soyuzmultfilm library. We digitally restored the film materials in Hollywood and had them revoiced by some of the world's best-loved actors. To date, two features and three series have been restored from the Soyuzmultfilm library, in addition to "Mikhail Baryshnikov's Stories From My Childhood."

The fairy tales and folktales included in this anthology were written, directed, and artistically conceived by some of Soyuzmultfilm's greatest talents. To name but a few, there are Ivan Ivanov-Vano (director of *Ivan and His Magic Pony; Pinocchio and the Golden Key; The Prince, the Swan, and the Czar Saltan;* and *Twelve Months*); Lev Atamanov (director of *The Snow Queen* and *Beauty and the Beast: A Tale of the Crimson Flower*); Ivan Aksenchuk (director of *Cinderella*); Alexandra Snezhko-Blotskaya (director of *The Golden Rooster*); Vladimir Degtyarev (director of *The Snow Girl*); Roman Kachanov (director of *The Last Petal*); and Mikhail and Tatiana Tsekhanovsky (directors of *The Wild Swans*). Art directors included the legendary Alexander Vinokurov, Leonid Shvartsman, and Lev Milchin. Among the leading artists were Fyodor Khitruk, Valentin Karavaev, Vladimir Pekar, and Roman Davidov.

When first produced by Soyuzmultfilm, a number of films won prestigious international prizes. After restoration, both *The Snow Queen* and *Ivan and His Magic Pony* were awarded prizes at the U.S. Film and Video Festival; and *The Snow Queen* and *The Last Petal* became part of the permanent collection of the American Museum of the Moving Image in Astoria, New York. The entire series received the Film Advisory Board's Award of Excellence.

Introducing the treasures of classic Russian animation to wide audiences outside the former U.S.S.R. has been a formidable task. But through these films, previously best known only to a very small circle of aficionados, the richness of Russian culture has for the first time entered millions of homes from Los Angeles to New York to Paris to Istanbul to Tokyo. And the warmhearted stories and splendid art, created by dedicated and talented artists over half a century, have found a place in the hearts of today's children and their parents.

—*Joan Borsten and Oleg Vidov*
Los Angeles, California

Story Credits

Folktales are handed down from generation to generation and cannot be attributed to a single author, though particular versions may be. These credits include the direct textual source or sources that contributed to the film's creation.

Beauty and the Beast: A Tale of the Crimson Flower

The script for *Beauty and the Beast: A Tale of the Crimson Flower* was written by G. Grebner and based on a fairy tale by S. Aksakov. The animated film was directed by Lev Atamanov with art direction by Leonid Shvartsman and Alexander Vinokurov. The dialogue was adapted into English by Sindy McKay and features the voices of Amy Irving, Timothy Dalton, and Robert Loggia.

The Golden Rooster

The script for *The Golden Rooster* was written by V. Shklovsky and based on a poem by Alexander Pushkin. The animated film was directed by A. Snezhko-Blotskaya with art direction by B. Nikitin. The dialogue was adapted into English by Gary Stuart Kaplan and features the voices of Gregory Hines and Cathy Moriarty.

The Snow Queen

The script for *The Snow Queen* was written by G. Grebner, L. Atamanov, and N. Erdman and based on a fairy tale by Hans Christian Andersen. The animated film was directed by L. Atamanov with art direction by Leonid Shvartsman and Alexander Vinokurov. The dialogue was adapted into English by Stephanie J. Mathison and features the voices of Kathleen Turner, Kirsten Dunst, Mickey Rooney, and Laura San Giacomo.

The Last Petal

The script for *The Last Petal* was written by R. Kachanov and based on *The Little Flower of Seven Colors* by V. Kataev. The animated film was directed by R. Kachanov with art direction by K. Karpov and Elena Prorokova. The dialogue was adapted into English by Valerie Allen and features the voices of Kathleen Turner, Lacey Chabert, and Malachi Pearson.

Cinderella

The script for *Cinderella* was written by A. Sazhin and based on a fairy tale by Charles Perrault. The animated film was directed by Ivan Aksenchuk with art direction by G. Shakitskaya. The dialogue was adapted into English by Celeste Mari Pustilnik and features the voice of Sarah Jessica Parker as the narrator.

The Prince, the Swan, and the Czar Saltan

The script for *The Prince, the Swan, and the Czar Saltan* was written and directed by I. Ivanov-Vano and L. Milchin and based on a poem by Alexander Pushkin (known in Russian as *The Fairy Tale About Czar Saltan*). The dialogue was adapted into English by Sarah Woodside Gallagher, Judith Feldman, and Stephanie J. Mathison and features the voices of Jessica Lange and Timothy Dalton.

The Wild Swans

The script for *The Wild Swans* was written by E. Reese and L. Trauberg and based on a fairy tale by Hans Christian Andersen. The animated film was directed by M. and V. Tschenovsky. The dialogue was adapted into English by Mark Stratton and Lois Becker and features the voices of Cathy Moriarty, Danielle Brisebois, JoBeth Williams, and James Coburn.

Ivan and His Magic Pony

The script for *Ivan and His Magic Pony* was written by I. Ivanov-Vano and Anatoly Volkov and based on *Humpback Horse* by Piotyr Yershov. The animated film was directed by I. Ivanov-Vano. The dialogue was adapted into English by Gary Stuart Kaplan and features the voices of Rob Lowe, Hector Elizondo, and Daphne Zuniga.

Pinocchio and the Golden Key

The script for *Pinocchio and the Golden Key* was written by N. Erdman and L. Tolstaya and based on *Adventures of Buratino* by Alexei Tolstoy (which was based on the Italian *Storia d'un Buratino* by Carlo Collodi). The animated film was directed by D. Babichenko and I. Ivanov-Vano, with art direction by P. Repkin and S. Rusakov. The dialogue was adapted into English by Gary Stuart Kaplan and Valerie Allen and features the voices of Joseph Mazzello, Bill Murray, and Mel Ferrer.

The Snow Girl

The script for *The Snow Girl* was written by N. Erdman and based on a Russian folktale. The animated film was directed by Vladimir Degtyarev with art direction by Vladimir Tarasov and Arcady Turin. The dialogue was adapted into English by Stephanie J. Mathison.

Twelve Months

The script for *Twelve Months* was written by S. Marshak and N. Erdman and based on a European folktale. The animated film was directed by I. Ivanov-Vano, with art direction by A. Beliavkov, K. Karpov, and A. Kuritsin. Fyodor Khitruk was one of the animators. The dialogue was adapted into English by Stephanie J. Mathison and features the voices of Lolita Davidovitch and Amanda Plummer.